Beatrice's Fortune

Abby Richmond

Other books by Abby Richmond

Very Berry

Starring Eliza

Copyright © 2013 Abby Richmond. All rights reserved.

To all my friends and family.
Thanks for supporting me!

One

*All you need is love. But a little chocolate
now and then doesn't hurt.
- Charles M. Schulz*

My alarm clock starts beeping in my ear.

I roll over to turn it off. Ugh. I forgot I needed to wake up earlier today. I have a customer who needs what they ordered by later today, and I didn't have time to make it last night.

I scan the note my customer left me that instructs me on how the fortune-teller should look. My customer this time is Addison Parker, one of my friends from school. Her note informs me she wants the fortune-teller to be jumbo size (she promised she'd pay me the next day) and needs to be blue, which is her mom's favorite color. It's her mom's birthday tomorrow, and Addison needs a quick, inexpensive present.

I cut a piece of light blue paper into a perfect square. I fold and crease, fold and crease, until the paper forms into what I've made a million times before. I inspect my neat row of metallic pens and choose one of the nicest, the one that writes in deep sapphire ink. While I make the fortune-teller, my dog, Ivy, licks my toes.

Yes, my business is making and selling fortune-tellers. I know it sounds really, incredibly stupid, but it's a lot of fun for me, and people love buying them. I even have business cards that I got for my birthday one year. I stick one of them in the fortune-teller as I finish. I make fortune-tellers so often now that I can whip one up in less than two minutes.

New fortunes to use are always running through my mind. I've never run out of little messages to write in my fortune-tellers. Ever.

I cap the blue pen and put it back with my fortune-teller supplies. I get dressed, brush my teeth, wash my face, and eat breakfast in a hurry. The bus will be here soon, and even though I woke up earlier this morning, I know I'll just barely make it. I always just barely make the bus, no matter how hard I try to be on time. It's sort of, almost, a part of me.

My older sister, Nell, grins at me as she walks out the door before I do. I stick my tongue out at her. Most of my friends don't get along well with their siblings, but Nell and I are only a year apart and we almost never fight.

I don't fight much with Cody, either, my brother in kindergarten. He's just too sweet. Cody's really shy and quiet. Today, his light brownish hair is sticking up in the back and his green-gray eyes are droopy. He always looks like that right after he wakes up. Cody gives me a hug before I leave. "Love you, Cody," I say, shout goodbye to my parents, and fly out the door.

When I am on the bus, I sit down next to one of my best friends, Quinn Walters.

"Hey," she says as I slide in next to her. "What's up?"

"Not much. What about you?"

Quinn frowns. "My morning started out okay. I had a really good cinnamon bun for breakfast, fresh from Emeline's. But then it was all ruined."

Did I mention my best friend is a little bit melodramatic?

"Ashlie said she thought my shoes looked tacky." Quinn glances down at her bright pink sneakers with the neon yellow laces. "I told her she should mind her own beeswax."

"Good for you. And by the way, I love your sneakers. Don't listen to dumb Ashlie Cheese, remember?"

The reason why we call Ashlie Simmons Ashlie Cheese is a long story that begins at the first day of seventh grade.

The two us, Ashlie and me, were sitting next to each other in Ms. Paulsen's class because her last name started with *S*, and mine started with *T*.

I smiled wide at the new girl when Ms. Paulsen stepped out of the classroom. "Hi," I said. "What's your name? I'm Bea—"

"My name is Ashlie Bree Simmons." The new girl said each syllable slowly, as if I were a three-year-old and couldn't comprehend what she was saying.

She cut me off! If I were new, I would never act like that to someone who was trying to be friendly.

I tried again. "Well, hi. Um, I'm Beatrice Taylor."

"Your name is *Beatrice*?" Ashlie asked, incredulous. "That's so old-fashioned."

I winced. *She's new,* I reminded myself. *I should be kind and welcoming, even if she insults my name. She's probably just upset she had to leave her old school.*

"Yeah, well," I said breezily. "Anyways, welcome to Jefferson Middle."

"Do you have a middle name?" Ashlie frowned.

"Uh, no?" I didn't like where this was going.

Her forehead wrinkled in disgust. "If I had a name as ugly as Beatrice, I would definitely want a middle name to cover up at least some of the shame."

Excuse me?

I struggled for something to talk about with this girl. "Well, um, I have a fortune-teller business. You know, those cute paper things? I make them and sell them to people. This is my business card—isn't it pretty? I got them for my birthday one year."

I handed her the little white card imprinted with smooth turquoise letters.

Beatrice Taylor's Fortune-tellers
Email Beatrice @
beataylor@jeffersonmail.com

Ashlie smirked. "Fortune-tellers? Those dumb things that were popular in second grade? Who would buy one of *those*?"

Okay. She insults my name and insults my business. She is NOT just upset that she had to switch schools! This girl is plain mean.

I opened my mouth indignantly to reply, but Ms. Paulsen walked in right at that moment. "People, stop talking!" she said loudly, and we all fell silent. I glared at Ashlie. She glared back.

Later that day, I went to Quinn and told her how horrible the new girl had been to me.

"Bree?" Quinn said after I told her Ashlie's middle name. "Isn't that a type of cheese?"

"No." My breath shuddered a little, holding

suppressed tears. "I think it's spelled with an *I*."

"Whatever! Ashlie Cheese!"

She started to giggle, and then I started to giggle too.

So, yeah. Ashlie Cheese.

"I guess," Quinn says now. "I just wish she wouldn't be so awful sometimes."

"I know what you mean."

The bus slows to a stop in front of our school. Jefferson, the town we all live in, is right outside of Chicago, and the streets closest to the city can be really busy and traffic-y. On the bus, it takes around forty minutes to get to school.

Five minutes later, I'm in the halls of my middle school, stuffing my backpack into my locker. Except now I can't find my math book. Ugh. I have a tendency to lose things.

"Hey, Bea," Addison calls when she sees me.

Addison is really pretty. She's taller than me, with wavy strawberry-blond hair and blue eyes that always sparkle. She has a sparkly personality, too.

"Hi, Beatrice," she repeats. Addison grins at me. "Do you have my fortune-teller?"

"Yup." I hand it to her. "What do we have first today?"

Addison checks her schedule on her binder. "Double English."

"Oh, I thought it was math. Well, I'm glad

it's English instead." I really like my English class. We do lots of fun things that only enhance my love for language arts, especially writing and reading. Oh, and Shakespeare? Can someone spell out A-W-E-S-O-M-E-N-E-T-H? Har har. I'm named for a character in a Shakespeare play, *Much Ado About Nothing*.

Everyone makes little comments about my name that make me feel uncomfortable every once in a while. I'm sure no one really means to make me feel self-conscious (well, except for Ashlie), but still...I love my name, and really hate it when kids tease me.

"Yeah, well, luckily it isn't math class. Ugh, we got so much homework yesterday from that stupid class! I completely skipped an entire section because I didn't understand what the heck they were saying." Addison replies, and I finally find my math book and throw it in my locker. Addison loves math and is the sweetest person ever, but even she can't stand the teacher, Mrs. Hamilton. I stand up and adjust my binder and multicolored composition notebook in my arms. I tuck some paper and my purple metallic pen in my notebook, just in case I want to make a fortune-teller.

We walk together, dodging the rowdy sixth-grade boys. They are getting a talking-to by, speak of the devil, Mrs. Hamilton, the ancient, creepy, number-obsessed math teacher. Her freaky yellow eyes are narrowed, and she is wagging her finger at the poor sixth-graders while giving her lecture. I catch Addison's eye and we try not to giggle.

We arrive at our English class just in time. I hate being late. I've had really, really bad experiences with being late before, and they all involve Mrs. Hamilton. The skin around my fingernails turns pale, then turns red, as I clutch my binder and notebook tightly, remembering the times when I was late to Mrs. Hamilton's class. Let's just say that I never ever want something like that to happen again in my life.

I sit down at my assigned seat next to Erik Talley and Ashlie Simmons.

"Hello, people," Ms. Paulsen says. She grins at us. Ms. Paulsen is really nice, and she always has smiles for everyone in class, even the troublemakers. If I were a teacher, I would be stressed out of my mind, what with the hooligans in my class.

"Okay, everybody. Today I'm going to give you all a chance to start the project that I assigned yesterday. Take a laptop from the cart and start working. Remember, I expect you to write a paragraph about advice you would give to a kid who's being bullied. Go!"

Our school just got wind of this huge anti-bullying thing, and they're making the most out of it. This paragraph should come easily to me, since Ashlie is still bullying my friends and me, and it's completely unnoticed by the teachers, but right now I am brain-dead. I tap my pencil on my desk, racking my brain for ideas.

"Stop that," Ashlie says irritably.

I know what I'll write about!

Ashlie. Well, disguised of course, because I don't think it would go over too well with the teachers if I wrote about how mean Ashlie is to my friends and me.

"Sorry," I reply, glaring at her. I'm pleased to see she has typed nothing, because I just started my first sentence. Ha! It must be hard for her to give advice to a bullied victim, since she's never been a victim in her life. She's only been the bully.

I continue to type. What I'm writing is pretty good advice. I think. I mean, I hope.

It can be hard knowing that my group of friends is Ashlie's punching bag. Not literally, of course. She hurts us with her words instead of her fists. However, it's November now, and I'm used to Ashlie being snobby and rude and treating us like we're dirt. I won't accept any of Ashlie's insults anymore. I know how to stand up for myself and my friends. So, don't think of me as one of those wimpy characters you read about in books and see on TV. I used to flinch every time she walked past me, but now, I always either A, ignore her, or B, retort back. I know B isn't the best solution, but sometimes, I can't stop myself.

I continue writing my report.

After I've written about a page or so, the bell rings. I shove any loose papers into my shiny lavender binder. I skim the color-coded schedule that resides in the clear plastic pocket on the front of my binder and set off to go to...math class! I scramble out of the classroom.

●●●

At 3:07, I'm back on the bus. School is out, and Quinn and I are sitting in the same seats we sat on in the morning. Quinn is coming over to my house today, and I really feel like going to Emeline's to get some hot chocolate. It's a chilly November day today, and Emeline's cocoa is the perfect thing to go with that crisp pre-winter feeling.

Quinn and I unlock the door to my house. "Hi!" we both shout.

Cody comes to give me a hug, and he shyly waves to Quinn. I doubt there was ever a sweeter brother than Cody. He gives us a present—a miniature, gap-toothed grin—before he goes back to the kitchen to eat a snack. It's really a treat when Cody smiles that wide, because even though he is mostly cheerful, Cody is serious and quiet on the outside. On the inside, though, Cody is a little boy, and little boys deserve to have fun. He must have had a good day of school today.

"Mom?" I yell up the stairs.

Mom works from home. She is in charge of this complicated website thing business. And when I say complicated, I mean reaaaaalllllllly hard to comprehend. When I was younger, whenever someone asked what my mom did for a living, I would be at a loss for words. Heck, I *still* have a bit of trouble explaining her job.

"Hi, honey" is the distant answer that floats down the stairs.

"Mom, Quinn is here. Can we go to Emeline's?"

"Okay, but bring your cell phones with you."

"Beeeeeatrice!" I hear a squeal, and suddenly Sasha Reynolds is right next to me. Sasha is Cody's best friend, and she's, well, kinda obsessed with me. In a cute way, though. I didn't know Sasha was going to be at our house today.

I stifle a laugh when I think back to when we all first met Sasha at the local playground. It was a year or two ago. Sasha, a tiny, grinning, olive-skinned girl with long cinnamon-colored curls and a white and pink butterfly outfit, came right up to Cody and me, who were on the swings. She watched us for a while.

"Hi," I said, smiling at the teeny kid and nudging Cody.

And then she started chattering. And once little Sasha started chattering, there was no getting her to stop. "Hi, I'm Sasha. What's your name? Can I play your game? What game *are* you playing?"

I elbowed my brother, and shy Cody gave a small wave, his eyes on the woodchips below him.

"I'm sorry," I said. "Cody is a little shy, but he'd love to play with you, right, Cody?"

"Oh, I'm *never* shy," Sasha informed me.

"I can tell," I muttered under my breath, smiling.

"Huh?" questioned Sasha and Cody.

"Nothing." I couldn't hide my grin then.

Cody and Sasha are complete opposites—Cody is the most timid creature on the planet, whereas Sasha is really bold and outgoing for a little girl—but I guess opposites attract.

Now Cody wanders back into the foyer, looking slightly confused. I bet he was wondering where his friend had gone.

"Ohhh," he says, seeing Sasha, realizing that

she's here. Cody comes over to stand with Sasha, Quinn and me.

"Can Cody and I come to Emeline's with you, Trixie?" Sasha asks me excitedly, and the two kindergartners exchange eager glances.

Sometimes I think the name Beatrice has too many nicknames: Bea, Trix, Tris, and occasionally even Trixie. Okay, *that* one is really annoying.

"Another time, guys," I say.

Cody and Sasha retreat back to the kitchen. Cody walks the way he always does: the daydream-y half-walk, half-skip that is just so *Cody*, and Sasha strolls energetically, her long, thick curls bouncing on her back.

Quinn and I look at each other and start laughing.

I'm sort of wishing that I'd gotten my fleece hat from my bedroom once we get outside. I already have on my scarf and gloves, and of course my silver puffy vest, but the wind is way sharper than I thought it was before, and I know my ears are turning bright pink from the cold. Fortunately, Quinn and I get to Emeline's before I freeze to death.

Emeline's is my favorite shop in all of Jefferson. Emeline Smith, a woman who's in her, I don't know, mid-thirties, is the nicest person ever, and she always has great cocoa and great advice.

She is tall and slender, with a sleek dark blond bob cut and long fingernails that have a gold manicure. Emeline told me that once she got an offer from a fashion company to be a model in Chicago, but she turned it down because what she really loves best is being a successful *entrepreneur,* as she calls it.

"Hello, girls!" Emeline greets us as we walk inside.

"Hi, Em," I reply, and Quinn says her greetings beside me.

"The usual?" She grins at us, her hands drifting automatically over to the cocoa machine.

"Oh yeah." We beam back at her.

Emeline starts to make my usual peppermint hot chocolate and Quinn's pumpkin spice cocoa. We sit at the counter so we can talk to her while she works.

"Hi, Cleo!" I say, spotting Emeline's assistant wrapping a slab of coffee cake in brown paper for a customer.

Cleo Brinks, an African-American girl who's at the University of Chicago, works here a few times a week. She waves at me and brushes some of her curly dark hair out of her eyes. She always wears really cool earrings, and today she's wearing dangly ones that are shaped like apples and oranges.

"Beatrice, Quinn, how are you girls today?" Cleo calls.

"Fine, thank you," we call politely back.

"So, girls, talk to me," Emeline says, adding an extra pinch of sugar to Quinn's and my favorite polka-dot mugs. Emeline is always really environmentally friendly, and she rarely gives out Styrofoam cups if she can help it. She always asks customers if they need their cup of hot chocolate to go, and if they say no, she gives them hot chocolate in one of her pretty patterned mugs.

Emeline gives Quinn her cocoa, but she holds back mine. "I'll trade you for that fortune-teller you promised to make me," she slyly says to me.

"Of course!" I say, whisking it out of my puffy vest's pocket. In pink paper, with dark violet ink, is the fortune-teller I did indeed promise her a few days ago. She hands me seventy-five cents for the small piece of origami I made for her, and pushes the steaming mug toward me.

"This fortune-teller is for Margaret," Emeline tells us, her glossy hair swishing as she turns to put it in her purse.

"Ooh!" exclaims Quinn. "How is she?"

Margaret is Emeline's baby. Meg is seven months old now, and loves when Quinn and I babysit for her.

"She's good. She recently realized that Ross lives in the house too, and honestly, she crawls after him all day, trying to grab onto his fur. I suspect that she wants to ride on him like a horse."

We all laugh, picturing plump little Meg riding on Emeline's basset hound, Ross, like a princess on a pony.

This is what I like about Emeline. She has the best stories.

I slurp on the end of the striped stick of candy that is lolling in my hot chocolate. I take a sip of the cocoa, but cautiously, because it is still steaming.

"The hot chocolate is awesome as always, Emeline," I praise, and Quinn nods vigorously.

Emeline's voice takes on a more gentle tone. "Now, while we're on the topic of pets, how is Aladdin doing?"

I can't look at her. "He's lonely. He misses Jasmine. I can't say I don't know the feeling." I really hope the two of them don't notice the way my voice cracks as I say the last part.

Jasmine was my cat, and her brother is Aladdin. Jasmine and Aladdin were the best cats ever… and beautiful, too, both really furry with soft gray stripes. Jasmine went missing five months ago, and Aladdin and I miss her dearly. At first, I put up signs all over town, saying that my cat was missing, and what name she responds to, and my dad's email address. I even printed pictures of her. But after more than a month, when nobody emailed or called, my parents told me it was time to stop looking, and just pray that wherever Jasmine was, she was happy.

Emeline places her hand on my shoulder soothingly and hastily changes the subject, not wanting me to be miserable anymore.

"Did I tell you gals I got a new hot chocolate type? Imported from Switzerland. Mmm, Swiss cocoa is just truly scrumptious. Would you ladies care to be my first taste-testers? Free for my best customers," Emeline coaxes.

I look up. There is nothing I like better than when Emeline trusts Quinn and me enough to let us try new hot chocolate before anyone else.

Quinn looks at me and a grin splits her round face. Quinn shares the love of mine.

"What flavor is it?" she asks, wiggling and tapping her fingers on the spotless cobalt blue granite countertop.

"I'll surprise you girls," says Emeline, returning the grin. Quinn and I groan.

"Oh, Emeline…"

"Nope. But I think you'll like it." As Emeline turns to go to the storage room, her sparkly gold and blue bangle bracelets jangle.

She returns a moment later, nothing in her hands. "Close your eyes, and I'll bring you two the cocoa." We do as she says, eager to try the new inventory.

We hear the clatter of the mugs as she sets them down before us. "Okay, open them now."

Our eyelids flutter open. "Oooh!"

Emeline smiles. "I call it—*Bright and Early Cocoa.*"

I fix my eyes at my mug with interest. There is a half of a mini-waffle perched on the edge of the mug, the way they perch lime or lemon slices on the edge of a fancy glass at a froufrou restaurant. There are also multi-colored marshmallows from Lucky Charms cereal bobbing up in the hot chocolate.

"Oh, wow, this looks really good," Quinn says sincerely.

After we have finished our Bright and Early Cocoas, Quinn and I decide it's time to get moving. It's going to get dark soon, and the rule in both of our households is that if you're going out, you have to be back by dinner or else.

I push out my stool and Quinn does the same. "Thanks for the hot chocolate, Emeline," we chorus.

"No problem," Emeline twinkles down at us.

"See you!" we call as we exit the shop.

"Goodbye, Quinndle, and goodbye, Fair Beatrice," she calls back. I feel my mouth lift up into a smile. Emeline loves to call Quinn *Quinndle* because it sounds like the word Kindle, and Emeline owns a Kindle that she sometimes brings in to her store if business is slow that day. Emeline likes calling me *Fair Beatrice* because the character named Beatrice in *Much Ado About Nothing* gets called Fair Beatrice. Emeline's read tons of Shakespeare. She's very smart.

I wrap my bright multi-colored scarf around my head so my ears don't get that frostbitey feeling they were getting on the way here. Quinn giggles. "You look like a dork," she informs me.

"And *you* look like Kermit the Frog."

"What?!"

"I have no idea."

We start cracking up at my randomness, since Quinn isn't even wearing any green, and by the time we get to the road where Quinn and I have to go in opposite directions to get to our houses, we're doubled over in laughter.

"I'll see you tomorrow," Quinn yells as she walks the other way than me.

"Bye, Kermit!" I shout, the wind whipping my hair over my nose and mouth. Whether Quinn hears me, I don't know. We're probably too far away from each other at this point. I still holler it in her direction anyway.

Two

Life is uncertain. Eat dessert first.
- Ernestine Ulmer

The next morning, I yank open my curtains, only to see—

"Snow!" Cody says gleefully, bursting into my room. "It's snowing, Beatrice!"

Snow? It's snowing in *November*? I can't ever remember that happening before. Still, I'm happy about the snow. I like snow as much as the next person. Cody leaves the room, no doubt going to let Nell know about the snowy surprise, even though she probably already knows.

I get dressed in a striped gray long-sleeve shirt with dark jeans, and push a silver headband through my short brown hair. As I tug my red high tops onto my feet, I rub my eyes tiredly.

I have to hurry to catch the bus, so I race down the stairs and wolf down my cereal. I go outside and walk with Nell to the bus stop that's on the end of my street.

It's snowing really lightly, and I have a feeling it will stop in an hour or so. Nonetheless, there are still snowflakes dotting Nell's long, curly dark hair, and I know my head must be covered in snowflakes also. Nell rubs her hands together, shivering slightly. A few minutes pass.

"I wonder where the bus is," I say vaguely, watching my words come out in visible puffs from the cold. "Isn't it usually here by now?"

"It is," agrees Nell, "but maybe we should wait a little while longer. The snow could be making it late."

So, more time goes by. I hop around a little on the sidewalk to make myself warmer. After a bit, I pull back the sleeve of my jacket that's underneath my puffy vest and look at my watch. Once I get a glimpse of what time it is, I nearly pass out.

"Oh my gosh, Nell, it's seven-thirty!"

Nell's mouth drops open, horrified. "We were supposed to be on the bus at seven-o-five!" she exclaims.

We scramble back to the house, not wanting to be any later to school than we know we already will be.

"Mom! Dad!" we pant as we fling open the front door.

"Girls?" Mom strolls into the foyer in her pajamas, frowning at us. "Shouldn't you both be on the bus?"

"It...never...came...!" Nell chokes.

With a gasp of dismay, I realize my first class

is math today. "Oh…my…oh…my gosh! I have…math…first! Mrs. Hamilton…will kill me…"

Mom's eyes widen. "Goodness, girls, I had no idea! Dad has already left to drive Cody to kindergarten, but I'll…" She starts to mutter underneath her breath. "Okay, girls, stay in here and warm up for a minute while I go put on some clothes so I can drive you."

Nell and I plop down at the kitchen table, glancing at the clock on the wall every few minutes. Nell combs her fingers through her hair, trying to get out all the snowflakes.

Nell and I are really close, but we are total opposites. Nell is really pretty. She is tall, and has this permanent tan that I guess she was born with. I, meanwhile, am pale as the snow that's outside. I don't even have freckles. Nell's hair is deep brown and curly and thick and tumbles down her back in a way my straight, regular-brown hair never could in its wildest dreams.

Not to mention the big thing about Nell: She's a dancer. That is probably the biggest difference between us. I would love to dance, it's just that I'm really clumsy and I'm afraid to try in case I fall flat on my face. In ballet class, however, Nell looks like she's floating. In hip hop, she looks like she's on the edge of doing a split and then getting back up and doing a flip in the air. Oh, and I've actually seen her do that, by the way. In all her other dance classes—let's just say she exceeds limits in dance. Since I can't dance, I started to make fortune-tellers, and then, the idea popped into my head to make a business out of that, since I really loved (and still do) making them.

I drum my fingers on the table, and stare at the huge bulletin board on the wall of the kitchen. The bulletin board is overflowing with pictures and drawings that we kids have made over the years. Most of the drawings are by Cody. He really likes art and other crafty, creative things like finger-painting—yeah, Dad doesn't like that one as much as just plain ol' coloring—cutting up felt, making unique paper snowflakes, and shaping neon kiddie clay into miniature light-sabers from Star Wars. Once Cody is able to write more easily and neatly, I'm going to teach him how to make a fortune-teller.

I'm surveying a particular drawing of Cody's, a brightly colored castle with triangular red flags waving cheerfully at the top of the highest tower, when Mom comes down the stairs. Nell and I stand up immediately and all three of us race to the car. My book-bag spills as I run. My books, folders, notebooks, and binder slam onto the pavement.

"Ugh…" I bend over to pick everything up and cram it into my striped bag.

Twenty minutes later, we pull into the parking lot of my school. Nell and I say goodbye to our mom and jog together up to the second floor of our middle school.

I tentatively open the door to my math classroom. Mrs. Hamilton's sour, disapproving voice croaks, "Beatrice. You are exactly forty-eight minutes and seventeen seconds late to school, which starts at precisely eight o'clock in the morning. It is true that it snowed, but Jefferson received only a half-inch, also known as one point twenty-seven centimeters of snow. What is the real reason for your delay?"

Argh. Mrs. Hamilton has this weird thing where she only speaks in numbers. And to top it all off, when a student is talking to her, they must speak in numbers too—no excuses.

I hesitate, trying to figure out how to explain my bus mishap in Mrs. Hamilton's math language. "I ride the bus," I stammer, blushing, "and it was approximately twenty-five minutes late when I realized it must not be coming. It took my mom approximately five minutes to get ready, and approximately twenty minutes to drive us to school. Oh, that's all rounded to the nearest five. Um. So…yeah. Sorry," I conclude miserably.

From the back of the room, I hear Ashlie let out a tiny snort of laughter. Then I hear Quinn whisper furiously, "Be quiet, Ashlie!"

Mrs. Hamilton purses her lips at me, but doesn't say anything. I take this as my cue to sit down at my desk.

Fifteen minutes later, the bell rings, and I gather up my binder and math books and hustle out of the room, my face still aflame with embarrassment. Quinn joins me.

"You have snow in your eyelashes," she tells me, grinning.

I bat my snow-flecked eyelashes at her, grinning back.

"Did the bus come for *you*?" I ask Quinn, rubbing the snow out of my eyelashes.

"Yeah." Quinn looks worried. "I wonder why they didn't come for you and Nell?"

I shrug. "I have no clue."

"They must not like you," Quinn teases. "Or else they'd have come."

"Uh *huh*…that must be the case…well, I feel truly offended," I say in the same joking way, trying to sound very affronted. I can feel the bright red patches on my cheeks go back to their normal light pink as I laugh calmly.

●●●

At lunch, I make a beeline for my friends' normal table. Already sitting there are Addison Parker and Helena Rose Cameron.

"Hey!" Helena Rose calls. She tucks her loose auburn curls behind her ears.

I pull out a chair next to Addison and plop down in it. "What do you have?" Addison eagerly inquires.

"Um...PBJ sandwich, celery with cream cheese, a tangerine, and a pumpkin chocolate-chip cookie that I made myself." My friends and I like to swap lunches, or at least, part of our lunches. We've been doing it since second grade.

"Do you want my pomegranate seeds for your tangerine? You don't like citrus, right?" Addison asks.

It's true. I don't like tangerines. So I hand her the cold, firm citrus and accept the container of yummy, fruity, scarlet pomegranate seeds. Pomegranate is my faaaaavorite...honestly, what beats popping little juicy seeds into your mouth and waiting for them to explode? Not tangerines, that's for sure. I snatch a handful of the pomegranate seeds from the container and delight at the tart-sweet taste.

Quinn and Eliana Levin join us a few minutes later. Quinn takes a seat next to me and Eliana sits beside Helena Rose. Eliana is tanned brown, with thick black-brown hair that reaches her waist in a braid, and millions of string bracelets, rubber bracelets, and cloth bracelets up and down her arm. Eliana rubs her shoulders, covered in a thin cotton light-pink long-sleeve shirt. "I'm cold," she announces.

"Eliana!" we all groan. "Again? Really?"

Eliana moved here from Israel a few years ago. She's never gotten used to the chilly winter weather here in Illinois, and she claims that she's cold a few times a day. She still visits her Israeli friends and family every summer, and I'm suspecting she still hasn't adjusted back from her summer vacation.

Eliana nods miserably back at us.

"Here," says Addison, who's the kindest of us, "you can wear my sweatshirt."

Once Eliana is settled in Addison's navy sweatshirt, we're all giggling. Addison is much taller than Eliana, and as a result, the sweatshirt is way too big for her.

When it's time to go outside for recess, I push open the doors to outside. When a bitter wind blows, whipping my hair in my face, I realize with a shock of cold that I'm only wearing my light fleece sweater. My puffy vest is inside my locker. My eyes widen and my friends look over at me.

"What's wrong, Beatrice?" Helena Rose asks,

twirling her long ginger locks in her fingers happily.

"Left my coat inside. Be right back," I mumble, my teeth chattering. I go ask Ms. Paulsen if I can get it from my locker.

Pushing open the door again, a surge of heat envelops me and I give a relieved sigh. I race up the stairs, and once I get to the second floor, I arrive at my locker.

My locker has a label with my name and the school logo on the front, and a turquoise lock on the handle. I punch in my combination code and the locker swings open. All my decorations beam at me as I grope around for my puffy vest. I have a bunch of magnets hanging in my locker. Oh, there are the funny pictures my friends and I took at Rebecca Weinberg's bat mitzvah in September. I love the square magnet with the quote, "I have not failed. I have just found 10,000 ways that won't work" in green-and-purple letters by Thomas Alva Edison that is on one of my walls. There are more magnets too, most of them just plain round with patterned duct tape covering them to make them more interesting. The magnets hold things too, mostly little doodles my friends have made for me over the years.

I also have magnetic containers that I put spare pens and pencils in, a little purple magnetic mirror, and a small whiteboard that my friends write messages on with my squeaky black dry erase marker. I quickly read a note Eliana left me on my whiteboard—she wants a jumbo pink fortune-teller for one of her friends in Israel—and spot my vest underneath all the clutter of school supplies.

I retrieve my silver puffy vest and run down to the floor that has the door to the playground so I won't miss any more recess.

Once I'm back outside, I scan the playground to look for my friends. Finally, I spot Helena Rose's vivid curls and I run over to join them all at the monkey bars. Helena Rose is on top of Eliana's shoulders, gripping each bar as Eliana walks quickly to the end of the monkey bars and back. Quinn and Addison are sitting on a low brick wall that is next to the monkey bars, talking and watching Eliana and Helena Rose. My friends and I love to race piggy-back style on the monkey bars. I jog toward them, my feet crunching on the light dusting of snow, so I can join. Seventh grade is probably too old to be doing this, but we don't really care. It's just too much fun.

Quinn immediately stands up when I arrive. "Do you want to go on my shoulders, Beatrice?" she questions me. I hop onto Quinn's shoulders and grasp each monkey bar as fast as I can as Quinn sprints, full-pace. Quinn runs speedily, so I panic when her feet rush ahead of my hands and I'm still groping onto a monkey bar two feet behind where she's standing. I let out a shriek and she walks backwards so my bottom rests on her shoulders again. Once we're done racing Eliana and Helena Rose (we won) and my feet hit the woodchips below again, Addison claps. Addison doesn't really like the monkey bars, plus she's kind of too tall for them, so she just watches us when we feel like racing.

Helena Rose flips back her long curls and pretends to put on movie-star sunglasses.

"Thank you, thank you," I say, and take a deep bow, then curtsy for good measure.

"Girls!" a teacher whose name I don't know hollers. "It's time to go inside!"

Oh. Oops.

We walk towards the building. Addison walks next to me. "Trix, I gave the fortune-teller to my mom. She loved it."

I give her a big grin. "Great! I'm glad to hear that."

At that moment, Eliana trips, and she lands on Addison, who lands on me. I land on Quinn and Quinn falls over which knocks Helena Rose down onto the pavement. Her head hits the cement with a *thwack*! Oh no, oh no! I start to panic. None of my other friends seem to notice what happened to Helena Rose; they're scolding Eliana. I dart over to Helena Rose's side.

"Are you okay? What hurts?" I ask her urgently.

Everyone else realizes what happens and they look startled. "Get a teacher," I command Quinn, who runs fastest.

I watch Helena Rose sit up, my eyes wide with fright. "Are you okay?" I ask again. She glances at me quickly, and her face looks like she's about to cry. *No, Helena Rose, please don't cry, please don't cry*, I say in my head. I blurt out, "Look at Addison's leg!" to Helena Rose, hoping it will make her giggle again. Addison's leg isn't that funny, it's just that woodchips are clumped all over the leg of her gray jeans.

Thankfully, Helena Rose's trembling lips suddenly turn over in a smile. Oh, thank goodness. She starts to laugh shakily.

"Are you okay?" I inquire once more.

"My head hurts a little," she admits, "but I feel better than I did five seconds ago."

"Okay, good."

I help Helena Rose up and walk with her up to the entrance of the school building. As we pass the teacher, I say, "Sorry, false alarm." He looks like maybe he's going to laugh, and I decide I like him.

As we walk up the brightly lit staircase leading

to our floor, I can see Helena Rose's forehead swelling and turning a sickly yellowish-purple. Yikes. I try not to wince so she doesn't think that her head is already bruising and I can see it. She's not going to be that happy when she looks in the mirror later today.

Well. At least she feels all right now.

●●●

When I get home, I call up to my mom informing her that I've arrived. I march up to my room and do some homework.

Forty-five minutes later, I hear a small knock on my door. "Come in," I call out to whoever's knocking.

Cody appears in the doorway. "Oh, hi, Code."

"Hi, Tris," he replies shyly. He's clutching a clear plastic box full of Magic Markers. The box looks too heavy for him—it's lopsided in his arms and he looks like he's struggling a little. "Um, I was wondering, um, do you want to color with me?"

"Sure!" I drop my pencil and abandon my French homework. "Do you want me to carry this?" I gesture towards the box.

Cody nods and I take the Magic Markers from

him. I clutch his sticky little hand as he leads me to the den. He picks a spot next to the large windows and right in front of the radiator. He balances on his tip-toes and takes the box of Magic Markers from me. He sets it down on the wood floor.

I peek out the window for a second. It's still snowing, but the snow is much lighter now than it was in the morning. Only little flurries. The sun is shining brightly from behind a small, fluffy cloud.

Cody gets some white paper from our computer printer and sits down with me. Then he asks another question in his quiet, sweet voice, looking up at me with his huge green-gray eyes.

"Can we, um, use Mom's yoga mats and make, like, a cave?" He looks nervous.

"Definitely, Code. You got it." He smiles a relieved smile, his absent front teeth prominent. Cody walks calmly down to the basement, his black track pants rustling as he goes.

He returns with two thick blue mats folded in his arms. They're stacked on top of each other, and look kind of heavy. I start to rush over to him to take the mats from him, but he shakes his head. Cody's face is set in fierce determination. He's so adorable. My kindergarten brother, the little man. He finally opens his arms and out the yoga mats tumble.

We get to work building a wall around us. When I finish setting the tall bulky mats upright like a wall, Cody grins at me and I slap him a high-five. His face set in the same kind of determination as it was a few minutes ago, he jumps over the large mat. I applaud him and he looks happier than he has all week. I step over the mat to get inside the small enclosed space that we built. It's cramped, but if Cody's happy, then I'm happy. I'll do almost anything for my gentle, kind, bashful little brother.

I'm about to uncap a red marker and ask him what he wants to draw when he opens his mouth again. "Can we take another yoga mat and make a roof?"

"Maybe another time, Cody, okay?" Seeing the disappointed look on his face, I hastily tell him, "It'll be cooler with no roof." Luckily, Cody's face lights up again.

"What do you want to draw?" I smile down at him, giving his shoulders a squeeze.

"A castle, please?"

"You gotcha. Want me to outline it for you and we can color it in together?"

Cody nods, so I finally uncap my red marker and draw the outline of a sprawling castle with a drawbridge and lofty towers with triangular flags waving cheerfully from the top. Cody gets to work coloring in the drawbridge with a bright orange marker. I take a grass-green marker to color in a flag when Cody's arm bumps into me a little and my marker leaves a trail of green outside the red-outlined triangle. Cody looks at me, playfully reproachful, and his whole face crinkles up with the wideness of his grin.

"Oops," I admit, shrugging my shoulders, but my face is delighted. All of a sudden, I am so overwhelmingly happy. *Cody, my baby brother, is outgrowing some of his shyness.* I am so overjoyed and stunned that I just sit there for a moment, staring at my little brother.

He nudges me. "Tris?" He looks kind of concerned. "Are you okay?"

"I'm better than okay," I reply, squeezing his hand. "I feel great." Right at that second, we hear someone coming down the stairs, then entering the den, where Cody and I are located. "HIDE!" Cody hisses, unable to control his laughter. A second later, the yoga mat walls are plummeting down and when I look up, Ivy, my dog, is standing there, looking extremely pleased with herself for finding Cody and me.

"*Ivy…*" I groan. Cody goes over to rub her belly while I try to build our fort again.

None of my friends have ever seen a dog bigger than Ivy. She is humongous, though she'd never hurt a fly. She's very gentle and loving and loyal. She is a big chocolate Labradoodle, which is a cross between a Labrador and a poodle. We got her six years ago, when we decided we wanted more than two cats. We were a pretty large family—father, mother, daughter, another daughter, son, cat, another cat, and a huge dog—until Jasmine went missing. I guess we're still a large family, but it isn't the same without Jasmine. My happy mood evaporates for a minute or two as I think about poor Jasmine.

She has to be alive. She has to.

As I listen to Ivy's blissful panting while Cody rubs her belly, I think about what I can do to keep up the search for Jasmine.

Speaking of Jasmine. Her beloved brother, Aladdin, slinks into the room, looking haughty and, well, adorable. The sunlight from the windows makes his tufts of gray fur shine. But he hasn't touched his food in a day or two, and he looks thinner. And when I look at his face and his body expressions, they are all symbols that say, *I'm a sad cat. Please help me. I need my sister. I miss her. Help me find her.*

I will, Aladdin, I say back to him in my head. *I promise to find Jasmine.* And then I get an idea.

Three

Chocolate is the answer.
Who cares what the question is?
- Anonymous

I hate to leave Cody, but all of a sudden it's urgent that I go see Emeline. I leave him goofing around with our pets and holler up to my dad, who got home early from work today, that I'm going to Emeline's and will be back in half an hour.

Once I arrive at her hot chocolate store, located on Lincoln Street, I push open the door and march right up to the counter.

"Hello, Beatrice! What can I do for you today?" Emeline says pleasantly as I pull out a stool to sit on.

"Hi, um, so..." I trail off, starting to feel stupid. How can I explain to her my thoughts about Jasmine? In the end, I scold myself for not trusting her to take me seriously. "I need your help," I say, and to my disgust, I burst into tears.

"Oh, Beatrice!" Emeline says tenderly. "What's wrong?" She hands me a tissue from a peach paisley tissue box and rubs my shoulder as I let my tears out. Finally, I stop crying.

"Good. Now, explain to me what's the

matter." She pauses. "Actually, give me a sec." She hops up, and since there's nobody left in the shop, she turns the double-sided sign on the window from OPEN to CLOSED. She gestures for me to sit in one of the comfy, cushy indigo armchairs that sit in front of the large fireplace. She quickly lights a big, roaring fire in the fireplace and plops down on one of the chairs herself.

"Now tell me; what's up?" Emeline questions casually. Then, again, she stands back up and starts making me a cup of chamomile tea. I shoot her a curious look that plainly says, *you're making TEA and not hot chocolate?* She smiles gently.

"Hot chocolate is great for just about everything, but tea soothes nerves better," she explains, clasping tongs over a little pale blue porcelain bowl of sugar cubes. "One lump or two?"

"Two, please." As she drops in two lumps of sugar, I feel a rush of love for Emeline. "Thank you."

"No problem, hon." Emeline waves her hand. Once again, she slips into the chair beside me. "All right, so what's eating you?"

I take a sip of the sweet tea. Yum. I take another, and savor the way the sugary herb tea feels in my mouth. "I'm worried about Jasmine," I finally blurt out.

"So I see." Emeline looks at me, waiting for me to continue. That's one of the things I like about her. She never pushes me or makes me do anything.

"Aladdin, too. He hasn't eaten in a few days. It's not good for animals not to eat their food! It means…it means…" My voice quivers, thinking of an article I read in a pets magazine about how sometimes when animals stop eating, they can die. I let out a deep, shuddering sigh and drink some tea. Then I set down my cup and saucer, in case I start crying. I don't want to break Emeline's china and I definitely don't want to spill tea all over my clothes.

"I know, Bea," she says quietly, with kindness.

"Really?" I ask with anticipation. Despite my sadness, I really hope Emeline has a story to tell that relates to my situation. Emeline always has the best stories, and they always make me happy at the end.

"My dog, Barley, ran away when I was little, only six years old. My family put up posters and notices, and eventually an old man, such a sweetheart, called our family, informing us he had our dog. Everything worked out."

"I know, but we already put up posters!" I wail despairingly.

Emeline hands me another tissue and motions

for me to pick up my teacup. "Drink some tea, Beatrice," she demands firmly, but benignly, so I do so.

When I'm done, I continue, "No, but Emeline, we already put up posters. We left them up for more than two months! Nobody told us they knew where Jasmine was. What if she's...what if she...?" I stop, unable to finish my sentence. I can't say it.

"Tris, I know it's hard, but you just have to keep hoping, all right? I promise you, it will make things a whole heck of a lot better."

I sniffle and nod.

"Now, you need to think outside of the box here, squirt. What can you do to find Jasmine? Think hard."

I squint my eyes shut, forcing my brain to think, but nothing comes to mind. When I open my eyes, I look around Emeline's empty shop. My gaze wanders to the light blue walls, the four wooden stools with the brown cushions on top, the dark blue granite countertop, the five rectangular wooden tables with pretty chairs, and the wide dark blue sofa. Finally my gaze wanders back to the armchairs where Emeline and I are sitting, and the blazing fireplace. "I don't know."

"Try harder, Beatrice. You're a smart girl. I know you'll find a way if you just *think*."

My gray eyes settle on the countertop. Next to Emeline's big purse there is a copy of today's newspaper. I stand up abruptly, my mind whirling. "Emeline..."

She looks at me calmly, ready for whatever nonsense may come out of my mouth.

"In the newspaper...but—an advertisement ...although..." I babble.

"An ad in the newspaper?" Emeline is the only one who can understand me when I gibber like this, besides, strangely enough, my older sister.

"Yes, but—" I pause to drink some of my tea. I'm so lost in my thoughts that I don't realize that I've drained the cup. I put down my teacup.

I proceed with my idea. "Maybe I could do something to raise money to put in an ad? A big ad, one of those full-page ones, maybe." I play with the silver bracelet on my arm. Engraved on it are the words **HOPE WISH DREAM**. I love this bracelet. Quinn gave it to me for my birthday one year. I wear it at all times.

Emeline looks at me intently. "It's a good start," she says. *Thank goodness for Emeline.* Emeline is supportive of me all the time, but she always keeps it real. I hate it when adults start gushing or simpering when a kid says an idea of his or hers. Emeline thinks practically about everything. We're a good pair, because she thinks with her head (sense) and I think with my heart (daydreaming, constant daydreaming!).

"But you're going to have to think about how you'll make this money. Those big ads cost a lot, Beatrice," Emeline continues.

"Yeah, I know, but I can just keep selling my fortune-tellers."

"Bea. Let me ask you a question, okay? How much money do you make each day from that?"

"I don't know. Two dollars, three, it depends."

"I know, hon. That's what I'm trying to tell you. It will take a long time to get that ad in the paper if you only make two dollars a day. Selling fortune-tellers just to friends at school won't be enough."

"Oh, no, Emeline!" My face falls.

"No, no, honey," Emeline says as I start to cry again. Poor, poor Jasmine! "I was thinking maybe you could sell them at a public place, you know. Like, maybe my store?"

"What?!"

"You can sell your fortune-tellers at my shop. Lots of people come in here every day, and they're bound to notice a spunky, determined girl selling her handmade crafts."

"Emeline? Would you really do that for me?"

I ask, my eyes wide.

"Of course, squirt. We can set up a table in a corner somewhere."

"Emeline! Thank you!" Wow! This is so cool! I jump out of my chair and give Emeline a warm hug. Emeline to the rescue! She's my hero. Or, heroine, I should say.

Emeline laughs. "No problem for my favorite customer." Calling me a customer is kind of inaccurate. Emeline never even lets me pay anymore. That's another example of how nice she is, and what a special friend she is to me.

"I should probably go. My parents will be getting worried," I say, looking at my purple watch.

"Yes," Emeline agrees. She grabs a chocolate-cinnamon cookie from the counter and wraps it up for me. Yum! I love Emeline's trademark chocolate-cinnamon cookies. My heart melts once again with love for Emeline.

I wave goodbye as I step out of the shop, taking a big bite of my cookie.

Everything is going to be okay.

Four

*I don't drown my sorrows;
I suffocate them with chocolate.
- Anonymous*

I remember when Emeline told me her business story.

"I grew up in a teeny-tiny town," Emeline told me when I was eight years old. "I was always an adventurous kid, constantly craving excitement. But my wishes for excitement were in vain, Beatrice, since, as I said before, I lived in this little, quiet suburb."

I nodded and took a sip from my peppermint hot chocolate.

"When I was just around your age, my wishes were granted. Because into my little town came Carrie Malone, a bright woman with always a kind word to say to everyone. With Carrie Malone came her cupcakes—Cupcakes by Carrie, her small, warm cupcake store, to be exact. Carrie made the most spectacular cupcakes and muffins. The cupcakes were complete with beautiful, colorful frosting, yummy toppings, and lots of edible decorations. The muffins were always a delicious breakfast, filled with fresh blueberries or raspberries or bananas or even sweet strawberries. And with Carrie and her amazing cupcakes came something else—a cheerful glow that came to the town when she did."

I nodded again. "I think I would have liked her," I said, giggling.

Emeline smiled down at me. "She was really a great person. She was my closest adult confidante, since I was never that close to my own parents. She would always give me the pink cupcake with extra frosting, or sometimes the pumpkin-chocolate muffin that had extra chocolate chips. She brightened up my dull childhood. Like I said earlier, Beatrice, she always had caring advice to go with her spectacular cupcakes."

I thought for a moment, then said, "Okay, I get it."

"My childhood was not as happy as yours is, squirt," said Emeline. "Since my town was so small, I didn't have a lot of best friends like you do, with Quinn and Addison and Helena Rose and Eliana."

I looked up at her from my tall mug of hot chocolate. "That's too bad," I said sympathetically. Now that I look back on it, it's a miracle that my little eight-year-old self didn't blurt out something tactless.

"Yes," Emeline agreed. "I was very lonely,

since I was also an only child."

"Oh." I couldn't really picture what it would be like to be an only child. Nine-year-old Nell had been going through her bossy, show-off phase at the time. Cody had just been born, and he was always barfing on me or throwing things or wailing for no reason. My house was always in chaos.

"Yes, honey, I know you can't imagine it, since you have Nell and now you have Cody too. And let's not forget your two cats and your huge, lovable dog." Emeline laughed.

I gaped at her. Emeline was a mind reader! "But let's just say that when I was growing up, my house couldn't have been more different.

"But then wonderful Carrie came, and she became a friend to me. Almost like a second mother, since my own mom never paid much attention to me. Carrie would chat with me as she prepared cupcakes, would ask me about school, about my pet goldfish, Goldilocks—"

I burst out in giggles. "Goldilocks?"

Emeline twinkled at me. "Yes, Goldilocks." She paused, still twinkling. "It doesn't take much to make you smile, Beatrice. I like that about you."

I beamed proudly. Any compliment from Emeline was a huge deal to me.

"But Carrie made an impact, a fantastic impact,

on my life," Emeline continued. "I vowed to myself that when I grew up, I would become a businesswoman just like Carrie...the type of businesswoman who brought smiles to people's faces."

"And here you are," I said earnestly, still smiling.

"Yes," said Emeline softly. "Here I am."

On Friday night, I'm still thinking about that afternoon from years earlier as I start to fall asleep. Emeline does amazing things—not just with cocoa, but also with kindness.

And, just like Emeline told me she did once, I vow to myself that I will do amazing things like that too one day.

Five

If there's no chocolate in heaven, I'm not going.
- Anonymous

That Saturday morning, I walk into Emeline's with my dad, my older sister, and Addison.

I invited Quinn to come with us also, but her clarinet lesson had to be rescheduled for today because her teacher is going to be in South Dakota all next week. Can someone say *random*?

Luckily I adore Addison too. Plus, bringing four people would have been a little much, now that I think about it.

My dad is a tall man with thinning brown hair and a short brown beard. Not one of those weird long beards. His facial hair doesn't hang off his chin, thank goodness. He may look tall, but he's quiet. He's very, very smart and kind, though. He is a psychologist and always has really good advice. My dad's glasses make him look more a little more approachable.

Nell walks in gracefully just like she always does, looking calm and pretty, her loose thick brown curls jiggling a little on her back.

And Addison bounces along just as always, her long strawberry-blond hair twisted up in a ponytail.

Addie's always optimistic, and no one could ever find a friend more loyal or clever or sweet.

"Hello, everyone," Emeline calls out to greet us. "Nell! I haven't seen you in a long time. You're still going by Nell, right?" she asks. Emeline is referring to my sister's full name, which is actually Penelope. Nell absolutely hates that name, though, and refuses to go by anything except Nell. Not even Penny, which I think is cute.

"Penny sounds like a name for a horse," she had replied when I asked her why she wasn't called the more common nickname Penny rather than Nell. "Nell is a person name." She scrunched up her freckly tan nose.

Now Nell makes a face at Emeline, scrunching up her nose again. Plus, Nell came in here with me last week. But Nell knows Emeline's just kidding.

"And, of course, the charming Addison!" Emeline continues, and Addison giggles. "How is the lovely lass today?" Addison's cheeks turn pink with happiness at being complimented, but of course she doesn't say anything back because she is too modest to do that. Addison's definitely pretty, though. She's the prettiest in my group of friends, and we're always telling her that.

Emeline greets my father, then says hi to me. "I could never forget Fair Beatrice!"

"Doesn't 'fair' mean, like, pale and towheaded?" I wonder out loud. "'Cause I have brown hair…"

"No, really?" Nell asks in a *duh* sort of voice.

"Ehh," Emeline responds to my question, laughing. "Who cares? My definition of it is just pretty. Now, everyone, would you like to see what I've got set up?"

We all crowd around the long, low coffee table that's in front of one of the longer blue sofas. "I brought a poster-board and markers so we can quickly make a sign for people to see so they know what you're selling," Emeline explains, pulling up the sleeves of her peach-colored blouse and setting a light blue poster on the table. She grabs a handful of colorful Sharpies wrapped in a rubber band from her designer tote bag.

Nell picks up a magenta Sharpie and Addison randomly selects a cheerful lemon yellow. My dad takes a neon pink marker, and I grin at him.

"I've got some munchies for everybody," Emeline announces, and we all exclaim our thanks. I don't know about Addison, but Nell, Dad, and I didn't have time for breakfast this morning. It's still pretty early. I check my watch. 9:04. Yeah, normally I wouldn't even be *awake*, let alone eating breakfast. "Would anyone like some hot chocolate or tea?" she asks.

Dad wants some plain black tea, Addison wants to try the Bright and Early Cocoa, and Nell wants the raspberry hot chocolate. I get up to help Emeline prepare all this. After all she's done for me—*is* doing for me—I think I ought to help her out a little.

"Thank you so much for all of this, Emeline," I say gratefully.

"No problem, Bea," she replies easily. "Now, could you pass me a mug?"

After I'm done plunking little pieces of cereal in Addison's cocoa, I look at the cabinet that's full of tea leaves and select some tea from the shelf that has a label that reads: *Chamomile*. Emeline makes a crazy face at me and I grin. "What? I've grown kinda attached to the stuff." It's true. I have.

I let the leaves steep for a bit, add in sugar, and then bring everyone's beverage to them. Emeline comes over with a small plate that has little blueberry muffins piled artfully on top. "Yum," Nell says, plucking one off the tray and plopping it in her mouth.

I take a bright, bouncy green—my favorite color—marker and start coloring in the bubble letters that Addison outlined in turquoise. I'm pretty decent at art because I've been making fortune-tellers for so long.

My hair is in a ponytail today, but it's a short, curved, spiky ponytail because my hair is cropped so short, only up to my chin. I actually like my hair pulled into this spiky ponytail. It's cute. Hmm. Maybe I should wear my hair like this more often. I don't do much with my hair most of the time, except for headbands. Beatrice, the spiky ponytail girl. I like it. I laugh to myself at my silliness.

Finally, after sweeping all the muffin crumbs off the poster and drawing, it's done. My dad tapes it up on the wall, while Emeline continues serving early-morning customers and winking at us in between. Once I lay out my fortune-tellers, which I worked harder on than usual, we're ready.

Our first customer is a girl who looks about nineteen. She comes into the store with a patterned laptop case, a big striped tote bag, and a notebook. She has long, straight, glossy auburn hair and emerald-colored eyes. I wish I had green eyes. But I do like my wide-set brown eyes, cheerful and bubbly, the same color as Emeline's cocoa, framed in black glasses. The girl has on a long-sleeved brown V-neck, a cream-colored scarf, bleached jeans, and caramel-colored suede boots. She seems very...well, cool.

She sets down her laptop case, tote bag, and notebook on a small table next to the fireplace.

She strolls toward us. "Hey," she says in a voice that's soft and a bit hoarse, smiling easily. "I'm Gwendolyn. What's going on over here?"

Nell nudges me encouragingly. "Hi!" I chirp. "I'm Beatrice. My cat, Jasmine, went missing a while ago, and I'm still trying to find her. I'm raising money to put a big notice for her in the newspaper by selling fortune-tellers that I made myself."

Gwendolyn cocks an eyebrow, and I suddenly notice that she has a tiny silver stud pierced into it. Wow, hip. "Whoa! That's so great that you're doing this."

"Thanks," I reply, tucking a strand of my brown hair that escaped my ponytail behind my ears. I wait patiently as she inspects some of my fortune-tellers. After holding my breath for what seems like forever, she holds up a pale mint green one with deep, shimmering navy ink. "I love this one," she says simply.

"I like it too." *Genius statement from Beatrice*, I think.

"How much?"

I beam. "One dollar." Yes! My first customer!

Gwendolyn rummages through her purse and hands me a dollar bill. "Thanks so much. This is going to be great to use on my roommates. Can you tell me more about this project? I'm working as an intern right now for the Chicago Tribune, and they might be interested in writing a small article about this."

My mouth drops open. Emeline widens her eyes at me from behind the counter, and Addison gives a little squeal beside me.

"Sure!" I say breathlessly. "Um, yeah!"

"Well, thanks for the fortune-teller, Beatrice," Gwendolyn says, smiling, "and I'll keep you posted on the Tribune thing. I'm a regular Saturday morning customer, right, Emeline?" Emeline nods and winks cheerfully.

My next customer is a little boy of about two who reminds me of a younger Cody. He comes over to the table and stares, hiding his face in his hands. Aww, how sweet! I decide to be extra-nice to the toddler.

"Hi, mister," I say kindly, smiling down at him.

He takes one of his hands off his face and peers up at me with gigantic, innocent brown eyes. "Hel-lo," he whispers, his brow furrowed.

"What's your name, little guy?"

He thinks for a minute. How cute! "Jeremeeeeee," he says cautiously.

"Cool! My name is Beatrice. Do you want to play with some of these toys?"

Jeremy nods. I hand him a fortune-teller.

He folds and unfolds it curiously, and I let him. It would be cruel to stop this adorable kid. Jeremy's father comes over, says hi, and reads my sign aloud. "That's awesome! We'll take this one," he says, gesturing to the jumbo-sized yellow fortune-teller that Jeremy is clutching, while murmuring unintelligible words. The dad hands me three dollars, and leads Jeremy to the counter where he gets a miniature hot chocolate in a teensy cup.

All the snow outside has gone by now. Today is a very bright—and FREEZING—day. The sun is shining outside, but it's one of those times where the sun is determined to make us cold, sending fierce, chilly rays of light down upon us, glinting evilly. Customers start to flow into Emeline's shop, and I can see why. Today is a good day for a hot chocolate.

I get four more customers in the next six minutes—an eleven-year-old blond girl, a group of teenage girls, a quiet boy who seems around seventeen, and a girl with a wide, plastic pink headband who looks around nine, towing her second-grade brother to the store.

While they all make their purchases, I smile and twinkle at them and say thanks and act all charming. After they leave, I whirl around to my father. "Dad, what if we don't raise enough money?" I try not to have my voice sound panicky, but I can't help it. "We've only raised nine dollars."

"Beatrice, stop worrying. We've only been here for half an hour. We have a while to go before we're done for the day."

"In a nutshell? Chill out, Trix," Nell clarifies, tapping a soft drumbeat on the table with her hands. Addison laughs.

I stick my tongue out at all three of them, but inside, I'm still nervous.

●●●

Three hours later, I'm in my room with Addison, counting up all the money. With my calculator, though—I am way too lazy to do all that math right now. Addison intently writes down everything I tell her.

"Okay, Adds. Ready for the grand total?"

"Yup," she answers, uncapping her pink pen. So I tell her.

"Twenty-four dollars and seventy-five cents."

She jots it down. Once she's done, Addison looks up, carefully searching my face for signs of emotion. I sigh. Addison knows me way too well, but that's one of the reasons why she's one of my best friends.

"You're disappointed, aren't you?" Addison

asks, putting down the pen.

"No...well, I guess so." I run over to my white drawers and pull out my favorite silver gel pen. I start writing on the piece of paper next to the numbers Addison wrote.

"I need to get to this amount," I explain while I scrawl out five hundred dollars. "How will I get there if I make less than twenty-five dollars a day?"

"Beatrice, you can't give up after one day." She says it very seriously.

I whoosh out my breath again. She's totally right. After I tell her this, she smiles and wiggles her eyebrows. "Afteer all, I *am* ze all-powverrrrrful, mageecal Addison Simone Parrrrrrrker," she says in a creepy accent.

I laugh and shove her. "Uh *huh*. Right."

"Vot? You doubt my ability to turn you into a frrrrog?"

"Yeah, I suppose that's what I'm trying to say." I stick out my tongue.

Addie pretends to be outraged but then drops it. "Let's do something that will take your mind off of Jasmine and money and all the chaos, 'kay?"

I think for a moment. "Wanna eat popsicles?"

"*Popsicles?*" The shocked look on her face is comical. "It's twenty degrees outside!"

"I know that." I roll my eyes at her. "But we could pretend it's summer, and we could have a picnic in my room."

Addison ponders this, and finally relents. "Okay."

I can't help cracking a joke. "I can tell you're *warming up* to the idea," I say, and we burst into a fit of giggles. The best kind of giggles, the kind that leaves you wheezing for air when you're done.

Luckily, my parents are willing to let us eat in my room so long as we eat on a blanket and don't get any crumbs anywhere. So, we find a red-and-white picnic blanket in the basement and drag it up to my room. Along with the blanket, I bring up two cups of Fresca that my mom likes (it's the closest I can get to lemonade), a platter of sliced pickles, two little bags of potato chips, and, of course, the infamous popsicles.

"Ewww, pickles?" Addison wrinkles up her nose.

I make a face. "Hey! I love pickles!" And to prove it, I grab one off the plate and start munching away happily, smacking my lips once I've gobbled up the whole delicious thing.

Addison takes a grape popsicle, and I take a too-bright red one that tastes like watermelon. Yum. In between, I devour the chips and pretty much all the pickles, since Addison refuses to touch them and I worship them.

Suddenly, the wind howls outside and the

lights flicker. Addison jumps, and I know my already-pale face goes white as a ghost.

"Did you hear that?" I whisper.

"Yeah," Addison breathes, clutching her bag of potato chips. The thin plastic crinkles, breaking the silence.

It's only three o'clock in the afternoon, but it feels as spooky as midnight. I peek out my window and see that the sky is quickly turning from a pale gray to a deep ebony. Suddenly, huge, icy snowflakes start falling from the thick clouds. *What?* Ohhhh, this can't be what I think it is.

"Blizzard," Addison announces weakly, confirming my suspicion, and promptly starts crunching her chips again nervously.

I put on my brave face. "Hey, you never know these days. For all we know, this could stop in, like, five minutes."

Abruptly, the lights go out. Addison and I clutch each other, breathing heavily. After a few minutes of silence, I get up and peek out the window.

"Well?" Addison asks. She's watching me from her spot on the picnic blanket.

I squint at the glass. "Oh my gosh, Addie, I can barely see. There's white swirling around everywhere. That snow is falling fast and fur—"

"Girls?" It's Dad, Mom, and Cody. They're

standing in the doorway of my room. "We wanted to make sure you guys were okay," Dad continues.

"I just checked the weather, and it looks like this snowstorm is going to stop sometime around midnight," Mom says. "I'm sorry, Addison, but there's no way we can drive you home in an hour like we scheduled with your mom. Not in this weather."

"Bea, you know those pajamas that Aunt Melissa got you last year for your birthday? Those are really long on you, right? Maybe Addison can fit into them," Dad suggests.

Addison and I look at each other, and Dad's words sink in. We both start screaming and jumping up and down. Who cares that we lost power? Who cares that it's snowing so hard outside that I can't even see anything out my window? Who cares that we're having a blizzard in early November? I certainly don't, because this means that Addison is sleeping over!

"So cool!" Addison squeals. "We're snowed in!" We dance around my room and I run over to Cody and take him by his little hands and pull him into our dance. He rubs his eyes. Poor Cody. The howling wind outside probably woke him up from his daily forty-five minute nap. But he's grinning, because he loves the excitement. I hoist him up onto my shoulders and bring him over to the window.

"Do you see that, Codes?" I holler. "There's a blizzard out there!"

Cody cheers. "I love snow!" he shouts, as I bounce him up and down with my hands and shoulders.

"We do too, Cody!" Addison smiles at him.

A confused look comes over his face. "But...where did the lights go?"

My parents try to explain about blackouts, but Cody doesn't seem to absorb any of it. He's too busy eyeing the box of popsicles on the picnic blanket. I laugh.

●●●

The sleepover with Addison is a lot of fun, just like we expected. Since it gets dark early, we root around for flashlights in my house. We call Addison's mom to let her know that Addison's okay and that everyone is safe, and that we'll drop her off tomorrow when the snow stops. Addison, Nell and I play Monopoly by candlelight in the family room. Cody is drawing right next to us, using his favorite crayons. Since all we have for light are flashlights and candles, I bet that tomorrow morning, the supposedly brown hair on the soccer player Cody is drawing will actually be orange, and that the green uniform will end up yellow. The limited light distorts all the color in this room. My mom is reading the paper on the couch, and my dad is working on a crossword puzzle. Ivy is dozing by my side, and Aladdin stalks the room, circling around, watching everyone with a suspicious eye.

I roll a six, so I move my token, shaped like a top hat, six places. I land on Park Place. "I'll buy it!" I crow.

Nell, who's the banker, hands me the Park Place card. Addison rolls the die. Her poor little dog-shaped token lands in jail. "Ha!" I say.

"I'm glad!" she retorts. "I'm sick of having to pay rent to you."

I smile smugly and rifle through my fake Monopoly money. "Let's see—thirteen ones, eleven fives, fourteen tens, nine twenties, nine fifties, five one-hundreds, and *six five-hundreds.*"

Nell shakes her head, sending her curls flying. "It's a game of luck, Trix," she says, rolling her eyes, but still smiling. "Whatever, though, I give up. You win." She grabs her shoe-shaped token and dumps it in the Monopoly box. I pick off all my little plastic houses and hotels and fold up the board. Addison collects all the property cards.

After a slight mishap with Ivy knocking over a candle and nearly setting the house on fire, Addison and I get to my room safely to go to sleep. We're exhausted. Ivy follows close on our heels, curiously trailing after my purple flashlight. I scoop her up. Despite her massive size, I've gotten used to picking her up.

Addison sleeps on an air mattress on my carpet, and Ivy settles right next to me in my bed—she really is the sweetest, most loyal dog ever—and instantly falls asleep again, breathing long, happy doggy-breaths. Addison conks right out too, but I lie awake, thinking. The sleepover was really fun, it's true.

But I'm still worrying a lot about ever finding Jasmine.

Six

*Put "eat chocolate" at the top of your list
of things to do today. That way,
at least you'll get one thing done.
- Anonymous*

Snow crunches beneath my feet as I traipse over to Emeline's. I reach down and pick up a handful of the soft powder and squeeze it into a ball. Cody, who's lagging behind because he keeps purposely stepping on little icy patches to make footprints, is huffing and puffing. "Come on, you turtle!" I shout at him, and throw the delicate snowball in his direction. He makes an effort to catch it, but it doesn't work. The snowball explodes into white glitter as it hits his navy winter jacket. He brushes snow off his coat and sticks out his little tongue at me, hurrying to keep up.

"No more dilly-dallying," I tell him, "or we'll be late." The bitter winter wind bites my cheeks and ears. I shiver in my turquoise snow-proof coat—it got too cold for my silver puffy vest a long time ago—and pull my dark purple wool hat further down over my ears. When Cody sees me adjusting my hat, he tugs at his little red hat too.

Finally, I take Cody's hand and push open the shop's door. *Ahhhh.* Heat rushes back into my face and hands. Cody sighs in relief, and makes a beeline for the roaring, crackling fire that's going in the big fireplace. Of course, the shop is packed today. I set my big plaid tote bag down on the countertop. I made the bag a few years ago out of some old flannel winter pajamas, and I love its coziness. "Hi, Emeline!" I greet her.

She finishes preparing the fancy-shmancy, expensive, imported-from-Europe hot chocolate, and then heads over to me. "Beatrice!" she says, smiling and looking happy to see me. "I'm so glad you've arrived. I have a table set up for you, but first, let me fix you both some cocoa—you and your poor brother must be freezing!" Her eyes twinkle, and I look over to see Cody. His eyes are blissfully closed as he warms himself by the fire. People laugh good-naturedly at his adorableness.

"Peppermint hot chocolate, please," I say. I really do like chamomile tea, but I'm totally in the mood for some chocolate-y goodness.

"And for the little gentleman?" Emeline prods. She busies herself in getting out the mint candy stick and chocolate. Wow. I like her sparkly cerulean nail polish, which is kind of funny, since I'm sort of anti-nail polish. Except on Emeline, of course, since she looks great in it.

"His favorite is the Marshmallow Mania cocoa, Emeline, you know that." I laugh.

She grins again. "I was quizzing you to see if you were paying attention. Now, while I make your drinks, go set up your table, okay? Let me know if you need help with anything at all." She nods toward the same little coffee table I used a week ago. I lug my tote bag with me, and carefully unload all of my colorful fortune-tellers. I arrange all of them in rainbow order—first red, turning boldly into orange, then yellow, darkening into green. The green shifts to blue, and the blue suddenly deepens into a rich shade of purple. The purple gets paler and paler, until it has softly faded to pink. Next is gold, then silver, then black. It's beautiful, and it gets people's attention.

First up is a confident eight-year-old. "I'm Cassandra," she informs me, sticking out her small hand. "Pretty rainbow," she continues, nodding at the table.

"Thanks," I say, watching her as she inspects a bright pink fortune-teller with orange ink.

"What's your name?" Cassandra asks. She squints at the poster Addison, Dad and I made a week ago, which Emeline must have put up before I got here. "Beatrice?" she says slowly, but she pronounces it like BEAT-RICE. Oh, for goodness sakes. I laugh, and explain how to say it correctly.

"Oh." She tugs on one of her carrot-colored, frizzy pigtails. "My mommy gave me this," she reveals, awkwardly grappling for something in the pocket of her pink parka. Her "mommy" waves from an armchair in front of the fireplace. Cassandra pulls out a quarter and gently sets it down on the table, like it's a million dollars and she can't lose it.

"Okay, Cassandra. You can pick one of these," I reply, motioning towards some of the smaller fortune-tellers, biting down my giggle.

As little Cassandra takes her own sweet time picking out a perfect fortune-teller, I notice something peculiar. There's a line forming in front of my table. Yes, a *line.* Oh, this is so great! First in line is the man who ordered the super-fancy hot chocolate from Emeline. Second is a toddler boy, on the shoulders of his teenage brother. Hey, that's Talia, Eliana Levin's older sister, third in line! I grin as I catch a glimpse of Gwendolyn fourth.

Once Cassandra has picked the pink-and-orange fortune-teller, it's time for the fancy-shmancy hot chocolate man. Fancy-Shmancy approaches me. "It's my daughter's ninth birthday tomorrow, and she's having her party next weekend. She heard about these—ah, cootie-catchers, do you call them?—from her friend Caitlyn, who apparently bought one when she came into the store last weekend. Curly dirty-blond hair? Pink plastic headband?" he says, eyeing my table.

Oh, her! Headband girl who came in with her little brother.

"Oh, yes, I remember her," I say, smiling graciously.

"Well, my daughter wants some of these for her party-favors. She's having twelve girls over to our house for a slumber party." He sighs, and massages his forehead. "Can you just give me some of the fortune-tellers that you think third-grade girls would like and I'll pay for whatever? Oh, and Veronica—that's my daughter—wants one too. Her favorite color is, ah, *magenta*."

Again, I choke back a laugh. Poor Fancy-Shmancy. I had a sleepover party when I turned seven, and let me tell you, I still don't think my parents have recovered from that yet.

I select a big, pinky-purple fortune-teller for Veronica and set it to the side. I pick twelve other brightly colored jumbo fortune-tellers. Pink with chartreuse ink. Sky blue with silver ink. Lime green with purple ink. Silver with hot pink ink. Yellow with fiery orange ink. The list goes on and on and on, until I have tastefully chosen twelve cute fortune-tellers. I do the math in my head. Each jumbo fortune-teller costs two bucks. Okay...wait a minute, that adds up to $26.00! Just from one customer! I start to grin.

I notice Fancy-Shmancy looking at the fortune-teller I chose for Veronica. He's reading the teeny gold letters that I printed in my small, neat handwriting. "Be sure to eat monkey cereal every day to prevent wiggly toes," he reads out loud, then, surprisingly, chortles. "These are funny. I'm glad my daughter made this choice."

I nearly burst with pride. "Thank you, sir."

Next is the little boy and his teenage brother. "You've already made your choice, haven't you, James?" the older one says.

James takes his thumb out of his mouth long enough to say a slightly muffled "Yeth."

"Well, which one?" his brother probes, hoisting him up a little further on his shoulders.

"Want blue," James blurts out, jabbing his wet thumb at a blue-and-red one.

I laugh. "Blue it is, mister." I hand him the fortune-teller and the teenager hands me three quarters. They bounce away as James curiously starts to unfold the piece of paper.

Oh, look, it's Talia's turn now. "Hi, Talia," I say. "Where's Eliana?"

"She's in bed with a really bad cold," Talia

explains. "At first, I just came here to get a hot chocolate for myself, but I noticed your table—duh—and I'd like to buy something for Eliana as a get-well gift."

"Oh, that's great!" I say, and Talia starts rummaging through her pumpkin-colored Israeli purse. She finally pulls out a funky wallet made out of candy wrappers and brandishes six dollars. I gape.

"Can I buy six? I want to put them on her nightstand, so that they'll be the first thing she notices when she wakes up from her nap." Talia is still holding the six dollars, looking at me uncertainly. She combs her fingers through her thick, flowing black hair as she waits for me to respond. I break out into a huge grin.

"Yes! Totally! Make sure to tell Eliana to feel better!" I squeal. Okay, six bucks might not be much, but I have so many generous customers today that it's hard not to feel excited.

Talia picks a pink fortune-teller (Eliana's favorite color), an electric blue one, a lilac one, a neon green one, a lemon-yellow one and a bright red one. "Thanks so much. I'll tell Eliana you say hi," she says, and flounces off.

Now it's Gwendolyn! "Hi!" I greet her cheerily. I'm happy to see my "old friend"—and maybe she has news about my little article.

"Hey, Beatrice," she says, giving me a smile. She bends over to look at a fortune-teller, and her dangly gold earrings tinkle slightly as they swoosh forward.

"Can I get this one? The other green one I got the other day was lots of fun, and I'd love to buy another," she explains, holding up a fortune-teller folded with bright, strawberry-pink paper.

"Of course," I answer, smiling. She hands me five dollars. "Oh, these ones only cost one dollar," I inform her, giving her some change.

"I know," Gwendolyn explains brightly, pushing back her change, "but I like to donate to the cause. Oh, and I'll be able to set you up for a little interview sometime in around a week or two. How does that sound?"

"Awesome!" I blubber, clapping my hands together. Gwendolyn takes a sip from her hot chocolate, waves goodbye to Emeline and me, and leaves the store. I make crazy faces at Emeline while I wait for more customers. I'm so ecstatic that I can't really contain my energy.

An hour passes by. I get six more customers, and all of them are polite and friendly as ever. When the hour's up, Emeline is still getting lots of business, but business for me has slowed down. That's okay, though. I'm going to count the money I made today when I get home, but I know I made a lot today. This means I'm one step closer to finding Jasmine.

I pack up my stuff and go to the counter to say goodbye to Emeline. "Bye, Emeline," I say happily.

"Wait a minute, Beatrice," Emeline says. She disappears for a moment and returns with two wrapped cookies. "Fresh-baked chocolate chip," she explains with a wink. "One for your brother, one for you. No charge."

"Thanks, Emeline! You're the best!"

I drag Cody away from the fireplace, where he's been sitting this whole time making weird little-boy sculptures with some Play-Doh he must have snuck in from the house. I wave one last time to Emeline. Gripping Cody's hand tightly, I push open the door and am immediately greeted by the frosty air. Cody shivers beside me. I unwrap the cookies. "Here," I say as we walk, handing him his. "It's a chocolate chip cookie. Fresh-baked, Emeline says."

Cody's eyes widen hungrily and he immediately takes a big bite out of the huge cookie. I take a bite of mine as well. Yummm. The chocolate is all hot and gooey just the way I like it. Cody smears chocolate all over his heavily bundled face and mittens. An expression of sheer joy is on his face as he quickly gobbles up his messy cookie.

Oh, Cody. I laugh and eat mine up rapidly too.

We arrive back home around fifteen minutes later. Cody retreats to the kitchen for a juice box—apparently all that hot chocolate and the cookie from Emeline's weren't enough for Cody—and I hang up our coats. I pull off my charcoal-gray snow boots and put Cody's black ones next to mine in the foyer.

Once I've dusted all the dirty snow off my hands, I run up to my room, and grab my favorite, coziest sweatshirt. It's black, and says "CHICAGO" in multicolored block letters on the front. Yeah, yeah, I know, it's really original and all that. But really, all that matters to me is that it's cozy. The inside of the sweatshirt is warm and fleecy and soft. I pull the sweatshirt over my head and smile when I feel the fleece against my skin. I also take off my blue cotton socks, and slip on my green-and-white striped fuzzy ones.

I head downstairs in my sweatshirt and fuzzy socks, grab the money I made from selling my fortune-tellers, and traipse into the family room, where I plop down on the couch.

"Don't you look comfy," I hear a voice say. I whip around and there's Nell, curled up on the armchair that's next to the couch I'm sitting on. She's holding a book. Probably *Emma* by Jane Austen—that's Nell's favorite.

"Why are you here? Isn't your modern dance class right now?" I ask.

"Yeah, but it got cancelled. It's hard for the girls who live in Jefferson—which is most of us—to make it to Chicago in the snow." She jerks her head toward the windows.

"Oh, yeah, I guess that makes sense," I say. "You must be bored here." I know my sister well. She's really active, and sitting around in one place for too long makes her restless. I bet it's from all that energy she gets from dancing.

"So bored," Nell agrees, rolling her eyes. "You and Cody were off with Emeline, so I've basically been sitting here for the past two hours reading *Sense and Sensibility*."

"*Sense and Sensibility*?" I ask, surprised. "Not *Emma*?" I finish counting the money from today. $51.50. Plus the $24.75 from last time…that's $76.25. Hooray! I'm getting closer.

She holds up the book and shows me the maroon cover. "I decided to try this one instead today, but so far, I like *Emma* so much better." Nell notices the wrinkly dollar bills in my lap. "Hey, how much did you make today? How much more do we need till we can put in the ad about Jasmine?"

I show her how much I made, and then admit how much more we still need.

"Well, look how much you made so far. It's a lot. Don't worry, we'll find her soon." Nell's voice is soothing, not like her usual teasing tone. She comes over and rubs my shoulder.

"Thanks," I say in a small voice.

My sister abruptly stands up from the couch. Her curls bounce. "Hey...wanna go outside? I am getting *so* bored of *Sense and Sensibility*."

"Yeah, sure," I say, brightening. Which, of course, means that I need to go put on my snow gear all over again, but it's worth it. Because Nell and I have the time of our lives once we get outside, throwing snowballs, building little snowmen, making snow angels, and basically acting like little kids.

I can always count on my big sister to cheer me up.

"Thanks for this, Nell," I tell her.

"No problem, Bea." She smiles at me, and then lobs another snowball in my direction.

Seven

*Stressed spelled backwards is desserts.
Coincidence? I think not.*
  - Anonymous

Several weeks later at school, Ashlie keeps getting in my friends' and my way. I'm walking with Addison to lunch one afternoon when Miss Cheese blocks the stairs.

"Whoa, giant," she taunts at Addison. "Don't squish me, giant!"

Addison's cheeks turn red. I know that Addison doesn't like how she's so tall, even if she is really pretty anyway. She hates getting teased about her height. Poor Addison fiddles with her blond ponytail.

"Stop it, Ashlie," I snap. "We have better things to do than discuss this with you."

Ashlie sneers. "Like what, may I ask? Play with little cootie-catchers?"

I clench my fist in frustration, and have to bite my tongue—*hard*—to keep myself from saying something I'll regret. It doesn't work that well. "I'd rather have that as a hobby than have your hobby of being totally rude to everyone you see. Come on, Adds. Let's go."

Addison and I push past Ashlie. "Thanks, Trix," Addison says, smiling gratefully at me.

As we plow by Ashlie, I catch a glimpse of her face. She's looking at the ground, a hurt expression creeping up onto her face. *What?* This throws me off guard.

"What? Oh. Oh, you're welcome. Not a big deal," I reply to Addison, flustered by Ashlie's expression.

Lunch drags on, even though everyone at our table is chatty and animated today. Except me. I keep stealing glances at Ashlie's table, where she seems to be upset as well. She's telling her minions something, when she suddenly bursts out into tears. I blink, guilt building inside my stomach, even though I don't think I really did anything that bad.

When I turn back to my friends, I see Helena Rose juggling my Red Delicious apple, Quinn's bag of pretzels, and Addison's yogurt. "Hey!" I exclaim, laughing. It feels good to laugh. "Apple, please!"

Helena Rose pouts, but she's giggling. She's been extra-bubbly—if it's even possible for Helena Rose to get more energetic—this week because her nasty bruise faded away. She tosses me my apple. I rub it against my shirt and chomp into it. I usually like apples, but this is an unexpectedly bad one.

I can't keep my mind off Ashlie. *I wonder what happened.*

At recess, I go up to her. She's sitting in a corner all by herself, shivering. She must have forgotten to bring her coat down to lunch.

"Ashlie—" I start, but she cuts me off.

"Save it for someone who cares, Beatrice." Her voice is sharp. "Go away."

I cringe. So much for feeling sorry for Ashlie Cheese. I spin on my heels and walk away.

But something about this whole situation is nagging at me.

●●●

As I'm doing my math homework after school that day, Aladdin slips through my open bedroom door and looks up at me with big green eyes. He seems to be saying, *Can I please sit on your lap?* I scoop him up. Aladdin's been needing extra love these days. He hasn't been eating much recently, and we're all getting worried. He purrs softly and bats at the strings on my sweatshirt. I stroke his striped, furry ears. "It's okay," I reassure, more to myself than to my cat. "We'll find Jasmine." I keep petting him, and he slowly lays his head down on my lap and falls asleep. He snores little cat snores, which Jasmine did too. I first noticed it when we got them when I was six.

I drum my pencil against the table. I can't focus on the math problems on my homework sheet. My mind keeps wandering. As I gaze down at Aladdin, my mind wanders to Jasmine. As I think about school, my mind wanders to Ashlie. I huff out a short sigh of frustration and plow my way through the equations, trying desperately not to think of anything but pre-algebra.

Aladdin wakes up after half an hour. He purrs at me, and when I can't bring myself to look at him because I feel so guilty, he gives an indignant meow. He's always loved attention, and attention from me especially. He also has an attitude that clearly states, *If you don't give me the attention I deserve, then I'm not going to sit in your lap.* I laugh. He hops onto the floor, offended. He's obviously reluctant to leave me, though—he must be lonely without Jasmine—so he settles down onto my little purple-and-blue rug in the middle of my room, watching me carefully.

I'm finished with my homework, so I might as well do something productive. While I'm still on my math roll, I decide to check in on how much closer I am to putting an ad in the newspaper. I never got around to counting the money from last weekend. I retrieve the dollar bills from my desk drawer and begin counting. Ten dollars, twenty, thirty...I keep counting and suddenly gasp. This puts me over the top! Oh my gosh! My eyes widen and I twirl Aladdin around in the air.

I fly downstairs, Aladdin following me, and start shouting and blubbering. "Guys! Everyone! Hello! Guys, I've made enough! Jasmine! Newspaper! Worked so hard! So close! Find! Where's Dad? Need to start making! On computer! Advertisement! I..." I pause to catch my breath. Whew. Getting excited is really a workout.

Nell is staring at me, in the middle of a straddle pose on the family room rug, starting to grin as my words sink in. Cody is bug-eyed, obviously not getting what's happening. Ivy lets out a confused bark from her perch next to my brother.

Mom gets up from where she's working at the kitchen table and lays a hand on my shoulder. "Beatrice, this is so exciting! But you need to take a deep breath, okay? Calm down a little bit and explain *slowly*."

After I tell them all how I've raised enough to put in the full-page ad in the Chicago Tribune, Mom smiles and gently replies, "Dad will be home in a few hours. Why don't you let him know about the great news when he gets here?" I nod. She continues. "In the meantime, try to relax, honey.

Read a book, go outside, do some homework, or make a fortune-teller or two." I nod again, but I don't do any of those things. I end up in my room, pacing, for the next two hours.

●●●

"And...voila! We're done," Dad announces, clicking on a little green square on the computer.

I take a look at the ad my father and I just created. It's bright blue, and has a huge picture of Jasmine in the center. **HAVE YOU SEEN THIS CAT?** it asks at the top of the picture in big black letters.

Responds to the name Jasmine. Tabby cat with gray fur and darker gray stripes, green eyes, light purple collar with the name "Jasmine" on a heart-shaped charm. If found, please email beataylor@jeffersonmail.com.

"Looks good," I say. "How do we send it to the Chicago Tribune?"

"Let me take care of that," Dad replies. He sends a couple of emails and clicks on a few links. "There. All set."

"Thank you so much, Dad!" I hug him.

"It'll be in the newspaper in a few days or so." He smiles at me. "Are you excited?"

"*So* excited!" I exclaim.
Ready or not, Jasmine, here I come!

Eight

Save the Earth.
It's the only place with chocolate.
- Anonymous

The advertisement has been posted in the paper for almost a week now, and I haven't heard anything.

I grab my binder from my locker at school as I mope along to class, tears stinging my eyes. I don't know why I even got so excited about putting the ad in the paper anyway. It's like I thought that Jasmine would appear as soon as the advertisement went public. *Life isn't like a fairytale. Jasmine won't magically return to me. Face it, Beatrice. She's probably—*

NO! I cut off my negative thoughts, mad at myself. I need to keep a positive mind open about Jasmine. *I can't get anywhere with a negative attitude,* I scold myself. *I'm strong. I need to have hope.* I put a smile on my face, determined to be cheerful.

I check my schedule to see what class I'm headed to. French. *Ugh.* My smile fades. I have that class with Ashlie Cheese—a.k.a. the Wicked Witch of the West. The last thing I need is to see Ashlie's red-rimmed eyes and miserable expression that she's been wearing ever since that day she started crying at lunch. I have bigger problems to deal with than having a pity party for Ashlie.

I settle into my seat, stuffing my things into my desk. Madame Thompson writes down a long list of French adjectives and I copy them all into my shiny aquamarine French notebook dutifully. I glance over to my classmates, scanning them all with my eyes. My gaze falls on Ashlie. Surprisingly, she's looking at me too, an anxious expression on her face. Our eyes meet. Ashlie looks away, but she still has that worried look on her face that is completely different from the sad one she was wearing earlier this week, let alone the obnoxious one she wore before that. *What?* I think in frustration. *What is going on with Ashlie?*

When the bell rings, signaling the end of class, Ashlie corners me and grabs my arm. "Beatrice, can you meet me at my locker after school? It's really important." Ashlie's voice is low, and her tone is urgent.

I'm thrown off guard. Why does Ashlie need to see me? "Um, well, okay..."

"Good." Her voice wavers, and then she runs out of the classroom, just like that. I hurry along to my next class, extremely confused.

●●●

The day went by incredibly slowly, but now here I am, waiting slightly impatiently at Ashlie's locker. She's taking the longest time putting all her homework and books into her backpack. She is obviously stalling.

Ashlie waits until the last person has left the hall and breathes a sigh of relief. "Well?" I question. "What's going on?"

"I—I..." She lets out a shuddery sigh and can't seem to continue.

I wait for her to go on.

I will remember what happens next for the rest of my life.

She starts again, taking a deep breath.

"I...I have your cat."

Time stops.

I can't breathe.

My heart pounds uncontrollably, and I get a dangerous lump in my throat that means I might cry. The hallway is spinning.

Whatever I expected, I didn't expect this.

"Y-you?" I whisper incredulously, staring at her.

"Yeah." She says it quietly, and doesn't look at me.

"Are you sure?" I ask her fiercely. I need to be completely certain. "Are you absolutely positive?"

Ashlie reaches down into her jeans pocket and pulls out the crumpled ad. "I'm positive. Don't worry, she's completely safe and healthy. She's been living in my house since the beginning of the school year."

What? So many questions are brimming up inside of me. "Why…how…what…" I can't seem to find the words to describe my questions.

Ashlie seems uneasy, probably not knowing whether I'm happy, sad, mad, or something else. She doesn't seem to know whether to comfort me or not, seeing as we usually can't stand to be in the same room with each other. "Come over to my house," Ashlie finally blurts. "You can take Jasmine back home, and I'll explain everything. It's a long story."

My brain is teeming with thoughts. "Um, okay," I stutter. "Let me call my family first, though."

Ashlie nods, so I stumble to the next hallway, away from Ashlie. I dial my home number on my cell phone, and my mom picks up on the second ring.

"Hello?" Mom says.

"Hi, Mom, it's me."

"Oh, hello, honey. What's going on?" I can hear the clacking of a keyboard on her line.

I hesitate, not sure what to say next. "Look, Mom...I found Jasmine."

The keyboard noises stop. "Oh my goodness! Are you sure, Beatrice?"

I swallow. "Yeah." I try to explain what I know so far, and ask her if I can go to Ashlie's house so we can figure everything out.

"Of course. Do you need a ride home?"

"Um, yeah, I guess so." I run back to Ashlie, cup my hand over the mouthpiece, and whisper awkwardly, "What time should my mom pick me up?"

"Five thirty," Ashlie mouths.

"Five thirty," I report to my mom.

"Call if you need anything. Nell's at ballet, but Cody's here with Sasha. I'll let him know the good news, and I'll call your dad." Mom lets out a relieved sigh. "I can't believe you found her."

"Me neither," I reply. "Bye, Mom."

"Good luck, honey. See you soon."

I flip my phone shut and look at Ashlie. I take a deep breath. "I'm ready."

●●●

Half an hour later, I'm sitting on the carpet in

Ashlie's peach-colored bedroom. Ashlie's upstairs on the third floor, looking for Jasmine in her parents' bedroom, where Jasmine apparently likes to hide under the bed. They aren't here. Ashlie's parents, that is. Ashlie told me that her dad is at his office in Chicago, and her mom is out getting a manicure or something.

I feel really weird here. It's my first time at Ashlie's house, and it feels strange.

I reach out for the bag of cheese puffs that Ashlie handed to me before she went to look for Jasmine. "These are my favorites to eat as an afternoon snack," she told me, obviously ill at ease. It's creepily ironic that she gave me *cheese puffs*, of all snacks, since my friends and I call her Ashlie Cheese behind her back, but I'm glad she gave this huge bag to me. I'm actually really hungry.

I pop a couple in my mouth. Crunching noises echo in her giant room, and I shiver in my dark purple long-sleeved shirt. I reach for some more, and some powdery orange cheese lands on my jeans. I munch down on the cheese puffs, wondering when Ashlie will get back. It's kind of creepy all alone in this massive room, in this enormous house. Ashlie must get lonely here, spending all her afternoons by herself in her room, eating cheese puffs and doing homework.

The door creaks open, and I start. I see Ashlie

carrying Jasmine in her arms. My eyes widen. Jasmine sniffs the air, and I know she picks up my scent. She jumps out of Ashlie's arms and flings herself onto my lap, knocking the cheese puffs to the ground and spilling artificial cheddar dust everywhere.

"Jasmine!" I cry, and clutch her tightly. She purrs the loudest I've ever heard, and bats at my short ponytail. I stroke her cheese-dotted gray fur, finger the heart-shaped charm dangling from her lavender collar, and wish that I had thought to put my phone number on the back of it so that we could have found Jasmine much sooner. She slinks down in my lap, gazing up at me happily, lightly nudging my legs with her nose.

"I guess you deserve an explanation," Ashlie says from the doorway, and I glance up at her, surprised. I forgot she was there.

"Right," I say. "Jasmine, stop licking the cheese off my shirt!"

Ashlie throws a stuffed mouse in my lap, which Jasmine immediately turns to instead. "That should help," she explains.

Ashlie sits down on the ground beside me, grabs a cheese puff, and starts chomping pensively. Maybe she doesn't know where to begin.

After a minute, she tucks a bit of her dark blond hair behind her ear and says quietly, "You know how I moved here this year?"

I nod.

"Well, when my family and I arrived at this house, there was a cat on our doorstep. It was Jasmine. She had a collar with her name on it, so I knew she wasn't a stray with diseases or anything, but the collar didn't have a phone number or address on it."

I wince. *I am so, so, SO stupid*, I remind myself.

She continues. "So I decided to take her in until I found out who she belonged to."

I nod again, slowly this time.

"I don't even like cats. You're lucky I was so generous."

Oh. This sounds a little bit more like the Ashlie I know.

I know she isn't really telling the truth, though, because she watches Jasmine fondly as she bats at the stuffed mouse.

I smile a little bit. "Go on."

"So I took care of her, not knowing a single thing about who the real owner was, until about a week ago..." Ashlie gets a slightly sheepish look on her face. "Well, I sort of overheard you telling your friends about how you put up posters looking for your cat up until late August or something."

"Yeah..." I'm not really sure where this is

heading.

"Well, I moved to Jefferson only five days before school started, so any posters you might have put up were gone." Ashlie watches me with her pale eyes, trying to see if I get it.

I don't understand. "What does that have anything to do with—" I gasp. "Oh!"

"But it wasn't until a few days ago, when I saw the ad in the paper, that I was really sure that I had your cat." Ashlie reaches out a finger and strokes Jasmine tentatively.

There's a pause. Ashlie opens her mouth, then closes it, then opens it again. "I'm moving again, anyway. To Manhattan. It's for my dad's job," she mumbles, picking cheese puff crumbs off of her fluffy white carpet.

"Oh." I blink. Now I'm confused all over again. Why did I need to know that?

Ashlie rolls her eyes at me. "My new apartment building doesn't allow pets, Beatrice. So, what I'm saying is, you can have Jasmine back without any of those complications there are in books and movies and stuff."

"Um, okay." I'm not really sure how to respond, so "okay" seems like an acceptable answer.

The silence next is so loud I can't stand it.

"I still can't believe that *you*, of all people, had

Jasmine this whole time," I comment to get rid of the deafening quiet. And it's true. Ashlie Cheese— really, who would have guessed?

What I meant as a simple remark makes Ashlie suddenly flare up. "I'm not that awful, you know." She spits out each word so fiercely it makes me gasp again. She's gone from quiet Ashlie to furious Ashlie so fast that I'm shocked. Jasmine jumps off of my lap, scared from the noise. She looks alarmed, and I can't say I disagree.

"I—I…" I sputter.

"Yeah, you heard me," Ashlie retorts, glaring at me. Her eyes look like little discs of ice. "Have you ever considered that it might be just a tiny bit *hard*? Moving from state to state, just so my dad can keep his fancy job? Never getting to keep all my friends? I move from one end of the country to the other constantly. I'm lonely all the time. My mom gets stupid manicures all day and my dad cares more about his job than about his pathetic daughter. You and all your friends make fun of me behind my back. I've moved a bazillion times, each time losing every single friend I make. I hate it. You don't know how frustrating it is for me." Her voice rises to a yell as she shouts the last sentence. "You don't know *anything*, Beatrice!"

And with that, Ashlie promptly bursts into tears, runs out of the room, and slams the door.

I'm stunned.

Probably even more so than when Ashlie told me she had Jasmine.

I stare at the door, my eyes filling with tears.

I didn't know. A tiny voice whispers that sickening—but true—sentence to me, and I recoil in disgust.

I suddenly remember a quote Emeline always said to me when I was little— "Try to put yourself in someone else's shoes. It's not always easy, but it's the right thing to do." Yes, Ashlie's always been sort of mean to me and my friends, but I never once tried to put myself in her shoes and imagine what her life was like. It really is true that I never knew about her moving so much, but I should have known that she wasn't mean for no reason. No one is.

Jasmine looks at me with mournful cat eyes. I look at Ashlie's peach-colored walls.

After five minutes of sitting in awful silence, a thousand times worse than the silence before, I stand up.

I push open Ashlie's door, and Jasmine slips past me and hurries down the hall. I follow her. Jasmine finally stops in one of the smaller hallways in the Simmons' huge house.

Ashlie is hugging her knees to her chest, crying softly. Her back is against the red-and-gold wall, and her head is in her arms. Jasmine immediately leaps onto Ashlie and rubs her nose against Ashlie's wet, tear-stained cheeks.

Ashlie strokes Jasmine, her tears falling slowly onto the cat's fur.

I sit down on the carpeting next to Ashlie, letting her cry it all out. After her tears subside into small hiccups, I know it's time to do what I need to do.

Apologize.

I muster up every single scrap of courage I've got and say quietly, "Ashlie."

She finally gazes up at me, her face so ashen I can count every single one of her freckles.

"I'm sorry."

She closes her eyes for a minute, then opens them. "I know." She speaks softly. "And...I'm sorry too."

I then reach over and give her a hug. It feels unnatural and natural at the same time, but mostly it feels nice.

"Really. I mean it," I persist. "I was really awful, wasn't I? And you don't need to forgive me. Seriously. I was terrible."

"No!" Ashlie laughs shakily. "You just...you just didn't know. And honestly, I was awful too. I really shouldn't have made fun of you and your friends like that. I was...I was a bully."

I can tell those words are hard for her to say.

"Well, it doesn't really matter now. And you weren't a bully, Ashlie. You were misunderstood."

She smiles hesitantly, choosing her next words carefully. "Thank you," she finally says.

I reach over to pet Jasmine. "No." I shake my head, thinking everything over in my head. "No. Thank *you*."

Ashlie's face splits into a huge smile.

Epilogue

*"We'll be friends forever,
won't we, Pooh?" asked Piglet.
"Even longer," Pooh answered.
- A.A. Milne,* Winnie-the-Pooh

"Puh-lease pass the gravy!" shouts Cody excitedly, trying to be heard above the din, scraping the last bits of his orange squash soup out from his plastic kiddie bowl. When Mrs. Parker, Addison's mom, proceeds to do so, he pours a whole swimming pool's amount onto his little pieces of turkey that Dad cut up for him. Struggling to hold the big spoon for the breadcrumbs, he dumps a huge amount of Mom's yummy stuffing onto the turkey as well. Everyone laughs.

I've already polished off my big bowl of the spicy squash soup that Mom makes year after year, and now I'm digging into my huge plate of stuffing, cornbread, sweet potatoes, cranberry sauce, and vegetables galore. I'm not having turkey. Call me crazy, but I really don't like it. Never have. So, my parents and all our friends always make sure there's plenty of other food for me to fill myself up with.

Our house is decorated with orange, red and

brown paper chains (made by me) and glittery orange paper leaves (made by Nell), not to mention all the colorful drawings of things like pilgrims, turkeys, and cornucopias that are taped up everywhere (Cody's inventions). But it's not the decorations that make the house glow. The happiness and kindness radiating from the house make me feel like the sun is shining, even though it's nighttime, so it's dark outside. *Thanksgiving is my favorite holiday,* I think to myself cheerfully.

Our house is crammed full of people. We've never had a Thanksgiving this huge. We've got cousins, grandparents, aunts and uncles, Quinn and her family, Addison and her family, Emeline, her husband, Brian, and little Margaret, their daughter. We've even got Ross, Emeline's beagle, and Ivy playing with each other and getting in everyone's way, probably hyped up by the overwhelming smell of all the Thanksgiving food. Aladdin and Jasmine, together at last, weave through everybody's legs and eye the dogs warily.

All the guests have been to my house before—all but Ashlie, who was also invited. Ashlie's parents let her come by herself since she is moving to Manhattan soon. She's smiling as Nell, who has already eaten two plates of turkey, tries to teach her how to do some sort of jazz step. A few months ago, if someone told me I'd be inviting

Ashlie to our Thanksgiving dinner, I would have called them insane. Now, it feels right to have her here. She's moving in two weeks, and although I wouldn't exactly say that I'm going to miss her terribly, I'm really, really glad we made amends. I was wrong about her. She was unkind at first, but I didn't really give her a chance, like I should have. Looking over at Ashlie fumble over the dance step with Nell, giggling, makes me happy. I overhear Nell say, "It's a really popular dance move in the jazz studios in Manhattan, my dance teacher told me...It's from the twenties, and has a really interesting style to it...it's totally coming back. Audition at a studio in Manhattan with this move—they'll be impressed!" Nell flashes one of her trademark friendly smiles, and shows Ashlie another move.

Speaking of Nell, I recently realized that I've completely gotten over all my feelings of "not being as talented." I still love to make fortune-tellers. Nell still loves to dance. But I've also gotten over any fear of dancing that I had before...in fact, I asked my mom to sign me up for beginner jazz-dance lessons starting next month. I'm going to give it a shot, and if I don't like it, then that's okay with me. I'm still going to try! I've decided that I can be capable of anything I put my mind to.

Quinn and Addison are cracking up as they use a couple of Thanksgiving-themed fortune-tellers that I made especially for tonight. Addison is twiddling a brown one with gold writing on her fingers, and Quinn picks numbers until they get to her fortune. I crane my neck to see what I wrote—*If you're feeling daring, get up and do a turkey dance.* Sure enough, Quinn stands up, and parades around the dining room with her elbows tucked beneath her armpits and her knees bent. She sneaks up on Cody, and he bursts out in hysterical laughter as she squawks, "Gobble! Gobble! Gobbbbble!" Quinn winks at Cody with one brown eye, pleased. Addison watches from her chair, her freckled nose scrunched up as she smiles sweetly at everyone.

My parents look content and relaxed as they chat with relatives. My cousins crack jokes with each other, and continue to help themselves to the yummy food. My aunts and uncles help out in the kitchen, buzzing around kindly.

Little Meg is cooing sleepily from her perch on Brian's lap, and all the adults are fussing over her. They're saying how cute she is and how grown-up she looks, which is sort of contradictory if you think about, but it's still nice. When she falls asleep, the grown-ups decide it's time to start dessert. I sit up straight and grin at Quinn, Addison, Nell, and

Ashlie.

The delicious aroma of cinnamon fills the dining room. Even though a minute ago I didn't think I could eat one more thing, I'm suddenly ravenous. I fill my plate with everything, overwhelmed at the sight of pumpkin pie, apple tart, Mrs. Walters' pumpkin-cinnamon cookies, and sugary apple jam to top everything off. Oh, and hot chocolate. It's impossible to miss the huge amounts of hot chocolate from Emeline's that are being lugged to the table.

"So, Emeline, what types are these?" I say loudly to be heard over the din.

Everyone quiets down, and Emeline smiles at me. "Glad you asked, Bea. The holiday flavors that I brought are the pumpkin flavor, and that's my apple-cinnamon. I also brought, just for the fun of it, my Bright and Early Cocoa, and Beatrice's favorite, good ol' peppermint."

"Yay!" I cheer, laughing, and the aunts and uncles scramble into the kitchen to grab as many mugs as they can hold.

Emeline twinkles down on me as usual, and her sparkly violet bangles and big silver earrings jingle softly as she laughs with me, her blue eyes full of warmth. "Should we say what we're all thankful for?" she asks, and everyone agrees this is a good idea.

"I'll go first," pipes up Ashlie suddenly. "I'm thankful for friends," she says, and I beam.

My cousins make jokes, saying things like, "I'm thankful for turkey," and "I'm thankful for pumpkin pie." My aunts, uncles and parents are thankful for family, Nell is thankful for her dance lessons, and Addison and Quinn are both thankful that they're friends with me so they can come to this amazing dinner. I giggle and shove them. Cody is grateful for Magic Markers, Brian and Emeline are thankful for everyone in the room, and it's not really clear what little Meg is thankful for since she's still sleeping. Finally, it's my turn.

I clear my throat. "Is everyone ready for a pretty long list?" Everyone nods. I continue. "Okay. I'm thankful for friends, I'm thankful for Cody, I'm thankful for Nell, I'm thankful for my parents, I'm thankful for Ivy, I'm thankful for Emeline and all the help she's given me, I'm thankful for everyone else in this room, I'm thankful that we've finally got Jasmine and Aladdin together again at last, and most of all, I'm thankful for Emeline's amazing hot chocolate!" I grin, and everyone else laughs.

I cup my piping maroon mug of cocoa in my hands and tip it towards my mouth, delighting when I taste the familiar flavor of steaming peppermint and chocolate. I let out a big, contented sigh.

Emeline notices, and she winks at me.

The chatter starts up again, and I laugh softly to myself. Who knew Thanksgiving could be so noisy?

Aladdin and Jasmine slink to my chair and both settle down beside my foot. They start purring so loudly that I can even hear them over everyone's sound. I gaze at them, a smile nearly splitting my face. I reach into my jeans pocket and pull out a folded, slightly tattered newspaper article. My smile growing wider, I unfold the article. I lightly place it in my lap, and begin to read it to myself for the millionth time.

Beatrice's Fortune
By Gwendolyn Farrell

Beatrice Taylor, age 12, is just an ordinary middle-school girl. She has homework and chores, and she likes hanging out with her friends. She especially loves to have hot chocolate at Emeline's, a fun, upbeat hot chocolate store in Jefferson, owned by Emeline Smith, who is coincidentally a close friend of Beatrice's. But during this past year, Beatrice had something extraordinary happen to her.

Beatrice's house had always been full of

family. Her parents, her 14-year-old sister, Nell, her 5-year-old brother, Cody, her dog, Ivy, and her two twin cats, Aladdin and Jasmine, were always nearby. But last summer, Jasmine disappeared. It was hard on Beatrice, and she wanted to do everything she could to try to find her missing cat.

On one October afternoon, with the help of Emeline, she developed a plan to find Jasmine.

"I like to make fortune-tellers," explains Beatrice. "You know, those little paper things. I love creating fortunes and using colors and being creative. We came up with an idea that I could start selling my fortune-tellers along with Emeline's hot chocolate at her store. All the money raised from selling my fortune-tellers would go towards putting a full-page advertisement about Jasmine in the Tribune. That way, customers could get a yummy hot chocolate, buy a fun, inexpensive fortune-teller, and help me find Jasmine all at once!"

After a number of weeks, Beatrice raised enough money to put an ad in the paper. And there was success! A couple of days after the advertisement was published, Beatrice found out that Ashlie Bree Simmons, coincidentally a girl in her class at school, had been taking care of Jasmine ever since she spotted the cat on her doorstep. Beatrice and Jasmine were reunited at last. As the fairy tale goes, Beatrice, her cats, and her friends and family all lived happily ever after.

I smile as I finish the article.
Happily ever after?
I look around at my family and friends surrounding me, happiness enveloping me like a warm hug.
Definitely.

About the Author

Abby Richmond lives in the Boston area and is in the seventh grade. She likes to write, read, act, sing, and play piano.

Beatrice's Fortune is Abby's third self-published book. All proceeds from sales of *Beatrice's Fortune* are being donated to the organization Music and Youth Initiative. The selection of Music and Youth Initiative was inspired by Abby's love of music.

Abby's first book was *Very Berry* and her second book was *Starring Eliza*. All proceeds from *Very Berry* have been donated to the organization Reading is Fundamental, and all proceeds from *Starring Eliza* have been donated to The Nature Conservancy. To date, Abby has raised over $3,600 for these two organizations through sales of her books.

Please visit www.abbyrichmondbooks.com for more information.